Our Glass:

Falling Sand

Michelle,
Thanks for the Support.
Here is to new beginnings

L. Shelton

Thanks!
L. A. Williams

Our Glass: Falling Sand

L. L. Shelton & T. A. Williams

Our Glass: Falling Sand is a work of fiction. Names, characters, places, and incidents are the products of the author's imagination or are used fictitiously. Any resemblance to actual events, locales, or persons, living or dead, is entirely coincidental.

Published by:
AATA New Beginnings
Newport News, Virginia

10 9 8 7 6 5 4 3 2 1

First Edition © 2017 by L. L. Shelton & T. A. Williams

Ebook ISBN: 978-1-7321525-1-9
Softcover ISBN: 978-1-7321525-0-2

AATA New Beginnings, Newport News, Virginia

ACKNOWLEDGEMENTS

The completion of this undertaking could not have been possible without the participation and assistance of so many people. The Cover Design by JD&J Design LLC contributions are sincerely appreciated and gratefully acknowledged.

However, we would like to express our deep appreciation and indebtedness to all relatives, friends, and others who in one way or another shared their support, morally, financially and physically. Thank you.

1

"I don't know what the hell I am getting myself into."

—Sadie

The road was slightly curved, slipping over the hills disappearing deep between rows of foliage. The car was swaying between the lines becoming engulfed by the surroundings. The car was on autopilot because it was driving me! My life is a huge mess and has been for a while now. I didn't realize the road I just turned down was about to change my entire life. My life was like an hourglass, and it had just been flipped over. The sand in the hourglass was about to fall.

Pulling into the first available parking space I see, *slamming* the gear shift into park, pulling the hourglass keychain from the ignition, throwing it on the seat beside me tossing my arms over the steering wheel and burying my face deep into my arms, tears began to fall as my mind began to drift.

For the past two months, I have been living in Pulse, Virginia, a small town sitting at the base of the Blue Ridge Mountains. Local businesses were mostly mom-and-pop-owned except for the one factory in town that manufactured parts for computers and cameras. The Otis factory has huge metal smokestacks, spinning wheels and a towering building. It was located at the top of the ridge that dominates the town as if to say, "You would be dead if not for me." It was a quiet looking town, and I was looking for some peace and quiet in my life, a town that would help me forget all about the months prior to arriving here, a town where I could finally wash the hell off me. The name Pulse was what made me stop running and find shelter. It was fitting since I needed to find my pulse. I have been dead for a very long time. The tears were finally slowing, as my face was buried.

I whispered between breaths, "Jesus, Sadie! What are you doing?"

Then I heard a noise. The sound was muffled. I could barely make out the words.

"HEADS UP!"

I raised my head just in time to see a ball land hard on the car hood. I jumped backward and ducked my head all at the same time.

"Christ!" I blurted out.

I slowly opened the door and emerged from the car. I could see someone running toward me. I did not know this would be my first sight of a new beginning.

"Sorry about that. Is the car okay?" the lady said as she stopped in front of my car. She was out of breath, so she bent over and put her hands on her knees. Her breathing was rapid as she seemed to be trying to catch it. Her hair pulled back in a tight ponytail, little beads of sweat were popping out on her forehead. I was just standing there in a daze. This lady was simply beautiful.

"It's okay," I stuttered, finally spitting out the words. I couldn't take my eyes off her.

I was starting to feel the sand was about to fall.

The lady pointed at my hood. "Can I get the ball? The ball right there?"

I looked over, and the ball had landed between the wipers. Picking the ball up and softly tossing it over, a beautiful smile came across the lady's lips as she caught it.

She took a step toward me. "It's not safe here. Why don't you park over there in that parking lot and sit on the bleachers? I will come see you after the game." She tossed the ball once into the air, and a smile came over her lips again. This time her lips were slightly parted. Her tongue was rolling over the bottom lip. In the blink of an eye, the lady ran away.

After coming back to my senses and looking around my car, I realized I had driven to a softball field. I had no control of the car nor my life. The lady with the ball was just over the fence. Her knees were slightly bent, waiting and anticipating the ball. She has nice, long, dark-brown hair. The hair was laying down her back almost covering the number fifteen on the jersey. Just as I heard the crack of the bat, the lady turned her head, glancing over at me. She smiled. I felt a hot flush rush through my cheeks. A tingle rushed through my body as I tighten my legs together lowering my eyes because I didn't want her to see me watching but it was too late.

I could feel the sand about to fall.

A force drew me to the bleachers. I found myself sitting on those bleachers watching a group of strangers play softball. Unable to move or to leave, my eyes constantly found player number fifteen. In my hands, I played with my hourglass keychain. Turning it over, glancing every so often to see the sand fall…flipping it over and watching it start new, admiring this lady from a distance.

Engrossed in thoughts, I didn't realize the game was over. I heard something hit the ground, and someone was standing next to me. I heard a voice say; "*Hey*! Glad you stayed; my name is _____…" All other sound around me had gone mute.

The lady slipped her fingers around my wrist. My eyes followed her fingers. Pulling my hand toward her, she caused my body to step closer. Our skin was touching; her fingers had a soft grip. She was touching me. My eyes trailed up her arms, admiring the muscle tone, over the shoulders and across her collarbone. Slowly eyeing her chin then her jaw bone finding her moist lips, my eyes gazed at them.

"And you are?" the lady said as I suddenly had sound again.

Popping back into reality, "*Umm*… my name, my name is Sadie." I barely managed to mutter the words.

Then there was someone screaming across the field.

"HEY, MAXIE PAD! YOU COMING TO LARRY'S?"

The lady's grip tightens around my wrist, pulling me even closer as she yelled back. "YEAH…. I AM COMING, TRYING TO BRING A GUEST!" The lady smiled at me with her slightly parted lips, and her eyes never leaving mine. The change in her grip let me know the words from that other lady made her body tense, almost uncomfortable.

Oh my, I felt like the sand was about to fall.

My eyes lowered, and I swallowed a few times. Lifting my eyes, I found the words. "Did she call you Maxie Pad?"

"Yeah, she is a tall glass of idiot." The lady giggled at her words.

I smiled at her words and let my eyes follow the tall glass. Tall glass appeared to be close to six feet tall, short blonde hair, long legs and slim. The muscles in her legs could be seen even in the low light. Tall glass was watching me as she stood by the car with her arm draped over the door. Her head suddenly dipped when she climbed into a red sports car. The car was too small for a woman of her statue. Tall glass backed up slowly appearing to stop a few times. In my mind, I could still feel her eyes on us or were her eyes only on me? I watched as her car taillights finally disappeared down the curvy road that brought me there.

The lady standing beside me nudged me. "Max, that's my name. Maxine is my name, but everyone calls me, Max. Did you hear me earlier? Never mind. So how about it? Go to Larry's for some pizza and beer with me?"

"I don't know, Max," I replied.

"Sadie, I owe you for saving our ball," Max replied.

"I saved your ball?" I giggled.

Oh my, I felt like the sand was about to fall.

"See that sewer drain over there?" Max was pointing to the first parking lot I pulled into. "That parking lot is known as Big Bertha. Big Bertha has swallowed more balls than I have kissed women. That ball was destined to land on your car, Sadie."

"Why?" I asked.

"Because…you chose from all those parking spaces to park in that specific one."

My inner voice screamed out. She doesn't know I didn't pick that parking space. My car drove me there.

Max kept talking, "That ball was doomed to be Big Bertha's next victim. So…see, you saved our ball, and I owe you dinner."

Max stepped closer to me. I took a half step back. The sand was about to fall. Max bent over and lifted her bag, tossing it over her shoulder. She smiled. "Come on and follow me." She walked a few steps in front of me, holding my wrist, guiding me like a child. I couldn't stop my feet. I didn't want to stop my feet. Max was driving me as my car drove me earlier. I have no control.

Max placed me in my car and gave me that smile. "Follow me and if we get separated Larry's is on Fourth Street. Okay?"

The sand was about to fall.

How did Max know I would follow?

"Yes, my work is on Fourth Street." Why did I just say that? I asked myself. What am I doing?

My car was right behind Max's car as we pulled into the shopping center. The parking lot had huge potholes, and the shopping plaza looked like it was on its last leg. There was a bright neon light from Larry's Pizza House that lit the one corner of the dining area. Next to Larry's, there was a laundromat. There were three people inside the laundromat staring at the machines waiting for the circling to stop. A few doors down was a pawn shop. Then at the other end was an adult store. Two women were standing outside talking, leaning against the wall, the ends of their cigarettes bright red with every inhale and a ring of smoke escaping with every exhale. The smoke was illuminated by the lights as it raised and twirled above their heads.

My car swung into the parking space right behind Max. Turning the engine off, I sat there waiting for Max to come over. Max's body was wiggling inside the car from side to side then arching backward. It finally dawned on me that she was changing her pants. Max's car door flew open, and she came out with her pants halfway down almost tumbling to the ground before she caught herself. She was struggling with her jeans. When she finally slipped them up over her thighs, she jumped into the air giving them one last pull. Quickly zipping them, she left the top button undone. The trunk popped open, and she started walking toward the back of her car. Max pulled her jersey off revealing a black sports bra. My eyes trailed from her breast down to her belly button. Her belly button was perfect, just deep enough to slip the tip of a tongue into. My eyes continued down to that undone button. How could an undone button be so sexy? Lifting my own shirt up just enough to reveal my scar, closing my eyes for a moment before I exhaled, tracing a three-inch scar with my finger where my belly button once was, I jumped as I heard the trunk slam hard, my fingers fumbling as I pulled my shirt back down quickly. Max had let her hair out of the tie and was combing it. She smiled as she started to walk my way.

Oh my, it felt like the sand was about to fall.

She was at my door! She was opening my door. This was crazy! Max extended her hand out inviting my hand to slip into it. Placing my hand into hers, she assisted me out of the car. Slipping her finger upward she wrapped her fingers around. "You have sexy wrists" Max was smiling. That smile made her lips part ever so slightly.

Oh my, I felt like the sand was about to fall.

"Hungry?" Max asked.

"Didn't bring my wallet, wasn't expecting to go out tonight." My inner voice was praying Max wouldn't see through that lie. The truth was, I only had eight dollars until payday, and that was for gas.

"It will be my treat, Sadie. You are my guest."

Max stepped closer to me. Leaning over she whispered, "I owe you for saving the ball." Max turned and started to walk toward Larry's pulling me behind her.

The closer we got to the door, I noticed there were two women standing outside Larry's. Their hands were waving, and voices rose.

The smaller woman screamed. "FUCK this and YOU!"

"Stop being a bitch," the larger woman yelled back.

Max never turned her head toward them while pulling me through the door. Immediately, there was tall glass at the table with another person. Max wasted no time heading to them. Taking a deep breath, I prepared myself to meet tall glass. Max stopped right behind tall glass laying her hand on her shoulder.

"Zena, this is Sadie. Don't be a bitch and say hello."

Zena barely turned her head. Flipping her wrist, she said hey.

"Hi. Nice to meet you." I barely got the words out before Max pulled my body away.

"Sadie, this is Colby. Colby is my best friend and roommate."

Max made the introduction while pulling me closer to Colby and away from Zena. Colby was too cute, with his bright as the daylight personality.

Colby jumped up surprising me. "Oh, Sadie! Isn't you just the cutest with that light brown hair, gorgeous hazel eyes, and that figure." Colby placed his hands on my waist and twisted me around. "To die for. What are you, a size 4?"

"That's enough Colby. Don't scare Sadie away," Max said smiling.

Colby punched Max in the arm lightly. "Don't mess this one up woman."

As soon as Colby spoke the words, I saw Zena pop her head around.

My inner voice spoke up. What did Colby mean? Mess what up?

Max and I sat at the end of the table. Two more ladies joined us just as we were sitting. I recognized them because they were the same women from outside that I had heard arguing. The smaller one plopped down beside Zena. The small lady crossed her arms and seemed to be pouting. Zena wrapped her arms around the small lady and gave her a hug then a nudge. The bigger lady I also remembered from the ballfield. She was the catcher. The bigger lady grabbed a breadstick and took a bite as she sat down across from the smaller lady.

"Hey Tori this is Sadie," Max yelled across the table.

Tori was the bigger of the two; she waved with the breadstick in her hand.

Max then pointed at the pouty small lady. "Sadie, that is Lacey." The pouty lady waved then went back to pouting.

I leaned over and whispered in Max's ear. "Are those two okay?"

Max turned her face inches from mine. "They are… They…

Well, they are just… They… You get used to them."

Most of the dinner was filled with softball talk, and about a trip, the girls were taking the next day down to Hunter's Canyon. My thoughts were carrying me in and out of the conversations. My inner thoughts were mainly asking myself what the hell I was doing. I have never had thoughts of another woman but found myself unable to stop thinking about Max. Maybe I was just glad to talk to people other than my landlady and boss.

The pizza was just about gone, and the beers were low. Max turned to me. "So…who are you, Sadie?"

"I am the ball saver, remember?"

Max smiled, and she placed my hands into hers.

Lacey jumped up almost knocking the table over. She bolted out the door almost knocking the waitress over. Zena handed Tori something then Tori ran after Lacey.

"Zena, what the fuck?" Max yelled out.

"It is the Tori and Lacey show," Colby added.

Zena waltzed down to our end of the table. Zena put a chair between Max and me. She placed her elbow on the table. Her back to Max and facing me, she waved her index finger in circles.

"So, Sadie…do you always stick your toe in the water before you dive in?"

Colby gasped. "*Uh, Oh*! … Here we go!"

Max grabbed Zena's chair and turned it hard. Zena's back was to me.

"What do you want, Zena?" Max asked harshly.

"Don't play with me. You know what I want, Max," Zena's tone became softer.

Max closed her eyes and took a deep breath. She repeated her question as she exhaled, "What do you want, Zena?"

"I need your keys. Tori took my car to go after Lacey."

"Zena! How do you suppose I get home? I can't ride with Colby because he got dropped off."

Before Zena could answer, I just blurted out, "I will give you a ride."

"Yeah, Max, the toe dipper will be glad to give you a ride. I am sure you will enjoy it too."

Max tossed the keys to Zena. "Bye Zena!"

Colby stood up. He leaned over to me and gave me a hug. "Bye sexy! I'm sure we will meet again." He kissed me softly on the cheek and then turned and kissed Max.

"Let's go, Zena!" Colby pulled her arm. They both headed for the door. On the way, they stopped to give an elderly gentleman at the door a hug. I assumed it was the owner, Larry.

"I am so sorry Sadie," Max said softly as she laid her hand on my leg.

"It is fine, Max. Zena is definitely a tall glass of idiot," We both giggled.

The older gentlemen walked over. "Max, it's closing time."

"Okay Larry, pizza great as usual," Max replied.

"Anything for my ladies, Max." He smiled and patted Max on the shoulders.

My watch was reading midnight. Where had the day gone?

We pulled in front of Max's apartment. Max turned to me with that smile on her face.

"Come on the day trip with me tomorrow." Max stuck out her pouty lip. I laughed aloud.

"Max, I am not sure that I should."

"Please! Please! Please!" Max said.

She reached over and wrapped her fingers around my wrist. Her touch was so soft. My eyes lowered.

"Those lowered eyes are very sexy, Sadie."

My eyes raised slowly. "Huh…? What?"

"Nothing Sadie" Max pouted again. "Please?"

"What time, pouty face? By the way, you look like Lacey pouting?"

Max's pout became a big smile. "Be here at 9:00 am with a

bathing suit on and comfortable walking shoes. My apartment number is 207."

"Okay…I will be here but…"

While looking in Max's big brown eyes, the words slipped out, "I don't know what the hell I am getting myself into."

Max kissed my hand then my cheek and whispered softly into my ear, "Not sure what I am getting into either, but I can't stop."

Oh my, it looked like the sand was really starting to fall.

2

"*So…Sadie*, tell me how you slept or did you sleep at all last night? Was your mind filled with thoughts of Max? *hum mm.*"
—Colby

Can't sleep! Thoughts were filling my mind, and I was wondering what I was doing. Max was all I could think about, and I was wondering if she was thinking about me.

Oh my, I thought, the sand was starting to fall.

I rose early to prepare myself for the day with Max. My shower was longer than normal. There were parts of my body that needed a little extra care, especially, if I was going to wear a bathing suit.

BAM! BAM! The bathroom door was about to burst off the hinges.

Then the screaming started.

"YOU HAVE BEEN IN THERE LONG ENOUGH NOW. THE WATER AIN'T FREE, YOU KNOW?" It was the lovely landlady screaming.

"I am getting out, Mrs. Preakness," I replied as I heard Mrs. Preakness' receding footsteps. Mrs. Preakness was an older lady who dressed like the sixties. She always has a cigarette hanging from her mouth with the ashes looking like they were about to fall. Mrs. Preakness was a grumpy left-over hippie who seems to be lost in the past.

When I arrived in Pulse, I didn't have a lot. Trying to escape the hell so fast, there wasn't a lot of time to plan. Five hundred dollars in my pocket, a few pieces of clothes, a used car, and a lot of pain, that summed up my life's belongings.

There was a room for rent sign in a local diner called Lucy's. It was a pay weekly, and that would fit my budget, which was almost non-existent. It was just a place to stay; the truth was that you get what you pay for, a small room, no electrical appliances, and no kitchen privileges. The worst part was the bathroom. The bathroom was shared with two others. One woman who worked late nights wore a ton of makeup and cheap perfume. Her smell would reach you five minutes before she would appear. I was pretty sure she was a lady of the evening. The second person was a burly man with hair all over including his back. That was totally gross, and I gagged every time I used the shower after him. The truth of the matter, the room was just a roof over my head, and it was better than the hell I am running from.

Rushing out the door, it was around 8:45 in the morning when I arrived at Max's apartment complex. I sat in the car for about five minutes playing with my hourglass keychain before I got the nerve up to get out. Now, I was standing outside of apartment #207 for another few minutes trying to get the nerve to knock on the door in front of me. Finally, my fist lifted and knocked softly. There was no turning back now.

I thought the sand was starting to fall.

Colby answered the door in a cheerful mood. In my mind, I imagined him in the mornings jumping out of bed all smiles and giggles with no worries in the world.

Music was playing, and Colby headed to the kitchen. I followed with my heart pounding in my chest.

"*Come on in, baby girl.* I was making some sandwiches and Max is still getting ready. There is some coffee over there; please help yourself. I hope you like turkey sandwiches."

"Turkey is great," I replied. He just reminded me of my mother. She always called me baby girl.

I miss my mom so much.

Looking around, I made my way into the kitchen.

"Are there any coffee cups, Colby?"

"Oh, my manners, here you go." Colby handed me a cup that read, "Lesbians Lovers" in rainbow colors. I poured myself half a cup of coffee then sat on the bar stool and watched Colby make lunch. As Colby made the sandwiches, he would twirl around and sing. It looked like he was just enjoying life and he had no worries.

Colby turned around to me. He leaned on the counter in front of me. Colby blurted out. "*So…Sadie,* tell me how you slept or did you sleep at all last night? Was your mind filled with thoughts of Max? *hum mm.*"

My face went completely red, and there was no hiding it. I buried my face in my hands. Saying to myself, How did he know? Was it that obvious?

"*Oh…Don't be shy Girlie*! Trust me… Max walked these floors all night long." Colby pulled my hands away from my face. "I believe it was because of thoughts of you. Those thoughts kept Max up *all night and me too*. Today, I will be a walking zombie, but I have my camouflage." Just then, Colby put on the biggest sunglasses I have ever seen.

I laughed out.

"There is that laugh," Max said as she walked into the kitchen. Max kissed Colby on the cheek, "Morning, my queen." Max poured a cup of coffee and leaned on the counter across from me. She was smiling as she sipped with her eyes on me.

"You look sexy, Sadie," Max said with her mouth hovering over the cup softly blowing the hot liquid. Those lips make me want to suck on them. These feeling were new to me.

I had on my one-piece, bright orange bathing suit with a fishnet shirt and some short running shorts. I never said a word, but I leaned closer to Max, smiling while sipping my coffee. The room was silent. We just stared and sipped.

I thought the sand was starting to fall.

Colby said, "Oh lord, let's getting going before you two ends up in the bedroom, and I end up alone with Tori, Lacey and Z."

Colby started pulling Max away from the counter.

We all grabbed a handful of stuff. The cooler, towels, blankets and bags. Max made sure one of our hands was free, then grabbed my wrist and walked me out. "I will drive," she said.

"You got your car back?" I asked as I was wondering how she got it.

"Z dropped the car off earlier," Max said as she walked steadily.

My inner voice was asking all types of questions. Why was Z here? Answer: They were friends of course. What did she say about me? Answer: Nothing good. What did Z mean to Max? Answer: I may not want to know that answer. Shut up! I silently screamed at my inner voice.

Colby jumped in the back seat of the car with those big sunglasses on and the ugliest floppy hat. I slipped in and sat beside Max.

The car rolled out for our day trip. We were finally headed to Hunter's Canyon. This would be my first time going to the canyon. Today would be my first time for many things.

The sand was about to fall.

We parked down the canyon by the water close to where we were setting up a small camp. The plan was for everyone to hang out at the campsite, eat lunch and then the adventures would begin. After lunch, we would take a four-mile hike up the canyon. Then we would rent tubes and have the river bring us back down to the camp.

Everyone else was already there when we arrived. Zena brought a girl, and they were curled up in a hammock between two trees by the river. Zena and the woman were kissing and didn't see us arrive. Tori and Lacey were near the area that looked like a fire pit. Lacey was wrapped in Tori's arms, and they were kissing.

Tori heard our car doors close and jumped up to head our way. "Hey guys, need help?" Tori said as she started to grab the coolers. "Nice to see you again Sadie and sorry about the stuff that happened between me and Lacey last night. You know how true love can be."

I just smiled.

Max put our stuff under a rock overhang about fifty feet from the river. She laid our blanket out and plopped down on it. She brought a small cooler just for us. Reaching in it, she pulled out fruit, cheese and bottled water.

Max started tapping on the blanket. "Have a seat, Sadie." Max leaned back on one elbow smiling. I sat with my legs crisscrossed facing her.

"Want to play a game?" Max asked as she bit into a strawberry.

"I guess," I said reluctantly.

"This is how it goes. I will ask a question, and we both must answer, and then you ask a question and we both answer. You can go first, Sadie."

I took a deep breath and exhaled slowly, then I said, "Okay…but nothing too serious."

Oh no, I thought the sand was about to fall.

First question: "What is your full name?" I asked.

Max responded, "Maxine Faith Shields."

I stated, "Sadie Marie Jones."

Max asked her first question. "What is your favorite color?"

I answered, "Yellow." Okay, that was an easy question. Maybe I can handle this.

Max smiled. "Mine is blue, but I really am liking orange today."

A smile came across my face. She was a flirt. I asked my second question: "Have you ever loved someone?"

Max answered, "Yes."

I said, "No." What the hell made me ask that? I told her not to be serious. I am an idiot!

Max starred in my eyes for a moment. She must have noticed sadness there that she hadn't seen before. Max grabbed my hand softly. "That will change one day. This is the last question, so let's make it good."

Max asked me, "Are you happy?"

"I am right now."

In was thinking the sand was about to fall.

Max responded, "Me to Sadie. Now…eat up. We have a long walk ahead of us."

We shared more strawberries and cheese. We nicely declined

the turkey sandwiches Colby tried to give us. Tori seemed to be enjoying them when she wasn't enjoying Lacey.

Reaching into my bag, I tried to give Max a few dollars for the tubes. Max pushed the money back in the bag. "The tubes are free. I did some work for the guy who owns the rentals, and this is his payment."

We all gathered by the firepit and got our stuff together. Zena and the girl finally joined us. The girl Zena brought with her looked like a model. Zena introduced her to everyone as Lorraine. We all smiled and said hello.

Zena bumped me as she went past. "How is that water?" Zena mumbled under her breath. I looked over to see Max, but she was talking to Tori, so she didn't hear it.

The walk was uphill and brutal on the body. I am using muscles that I had not used in a very long time. Zena was leading the pack and dragging Lorraine, literally dragging Lorraine through the brush. Poor Lorraine was not dressed for this type of walk. Holding my wrist, Max guided me through the trail. Every now and then she caught Lorraine as she stumbled. Zena was not amused and just kept dragging Lorraine harder and harder. I felt sorry for Lorraine. Behind me was Colby and he was being pushed by Tori. Colby kept screaming that Tori was touching his ass. Lacey was bringing up the rear. Lacey was in great shape and was not having any problems mastering the trail. She was being held up by all of us.

Reaching the top, we took a breather before jumping into the tubes. We had on life preservers because that was one of the requirements. They were far from fashionable. The water was cool and flowing slowly but steadily. Rocks emerged every so often above the waterline. We were warned to be careful of the rocks and to stay away from them. We were not connected but couples paired up, holding hands as the river moved us down the canyon. Max grabbed my wrist and pulled my tube closer to her tube.

Colby ambushed Max from behind, splashing Max with water

wetting her entire back.

Max screamed, "UGH, Colby! You little BITCH, come here!"

Max let go of my hand and chased Colby with the tube. I sat back laughing at the two of them; they looked so comical. Colby was a lot faster than Max could ever be. We were now close to the camp with maybe a mile to go.

I felt a bump, and it seemed to come from behind, but I wasn't sure. All I know was that my body was now flying and I had no control. I could see Zena come past me on the tube just as I hit the water. My head dipped below the water but soon popped back up. My tube continued down the river without me. I tried to swim but I couldn't. Something was wrapped around my leg. The vest was holding my head up, but the water was pounding my upper body. My arms were waving and grasping at the water. I was trying to scream… "MAX, HELP ME," but with every word, I swallowed more water. My tube flew pass Max.

Max turned around and saw me struggling to stay up.

Max screamed, "TORI, I NEED YOU!" just before diving off the tube into the water. Tori was right behind her. It was an uphill battle against the current, but that didn't stop the two of them. Max arrived first, swimming around me and holding me up. Max was pulling hard as she was trying to free me, but something was stopping her.

In my ear, Max calmly said, "Hold on…. We got you."

The water was pounding. My heart was racing as I began to feel tired. I swallowed water every so often, gagging for air. Max was struggling to hold me up, but she was refusing to let go.

When Tori arrived, Max called out, "Something has Sadie's leg. See if you can loosen it."

Tori pulled her vest off and opened a knife that she always carried. My eyes were wide open and filled with fear. Tori looked at me, took a deep breath; then she went under the water. Max held one of her arms to secure her. I could feel Tori's hand as she was feeling the inside of my thigh. Tori slowly ran her hand over my thigh to trace something that was holding me down. I felt the blade lying against my thigh then I felt a snip. Then it repeated. With every snip, I could move my leg a little more. The last snip must have set me free because I am able to kick out but I jammed my leg into the blade.

I yelled out, "OUCH!"

Tori popped up out of the water breathing hard. Max started holding me tight. Then she reached over and helped Tori steady herself. Colby and Lacey were fighting to get a tube to the three of us. The swift current was bringing us all together like puzzle pieces. Zena and Lorraine were onshore watching as the group fought their way back. We collapsed on the sand.

Max reached out touching Tori whispering, "Thank you." Tori reached out laying her arm on Max's shoulder.

Lacey ran over to Tori crying. "You scared me, honey." They laid in each other arms.

Max helped me over to our camping spot. Max gave me a towel for the bleeding. The knife only nicked my thigh. The bleeding quickly came to a stop after I wrapped the towel around it. I laid down exhausted with my eyes closed trying to catch my breath. Max jumped up. Max examined me over making sure I was okay. She told me to stay put, and she would be right back.

I could hear voices across the way, but mostly I heard Max. Max was asking questions to Zena about what happened. Zena sounded like she wasn't being cooperative and seemed to be getting mad. The next thing I heard was Zena's car starting up and peeling out. Trying to open my eyes, I could see Max checking on Tori and Lacey. Max walked over to Colby hugging him tightly. Tori's car started up, and the three of them left together. I closed my eyes and took another very deep breath. Max laid next to me placing her hand softly on my stomach. When I opened my eyes again, Max was leaning over me.

"Everybody is gone. So, when you are ready, we can leave too. I want you to stay at my place tonight, so I can make sure you are okay." Max said softly as she brushed my hair back. "Sadie, what happened? How did you fall off the tube?" Max asked again.

"I'm not really sure, Max. It may have been a rock in the river. I only felt a bump; then I was flying and..."

Max interrupted me. "If I find out Zena..."

Placing my fingers over Max's mouth, I whispered, "Just stop." I was touching those lips. They were so soft.

Touching Max's lips caused her shoulders to relax. Max reached up grabbing my wrist and kissing my fingers before pulling them away. Max whispered, "I have one last question for our game, Sadie, but I will answer first, then you."

"Sadie, have you ever kissed a girl?"

Oh my, I was thinking the sand was about to fall.

Max's lips were almost touching mine. Just hovering on my lips when she whispered "*yes,*" she wrapped her hand around the back of my head and pulled me into her. I could feel the softness of her lips.

Oh my, the sand has started to fall.

It has been a long, long time since my lips have kissed anyone.

Unable to control myself, a soft, low moan emerged from me over her lips. Max responded with her own low moan followed by her tongue slipping into my mouth and twirling around mine so gently. Then she pulled away very slowly.

Looking into Max's big brown eyes, my answer slipped out. "Yes...I have...just now"

Oh my, the sand was starting to fall.

3

"Who are you?"
—Max

Finally, back at Max's apartment, Max started fumbling with the keys to unlock the door. Her arm suddenly wrapped around my waist. Pulling me closer, she laid her forehead on mine. Her grip was tight around my waist like she was afraid I am going to get away. We just stood there with our eyes closed and synchronized breaths. The tension in Max's body was radiating through her pours. Everything that had happened earlier was finally overwhelming her.

I ran my hands over Max's shoulders and around her neck, running my fingers through the back of her hair. The tension started to dissipate, and Max's body started to relax. I stepped closer to Max and whispered in her ear. "Max, I am okay. Everyone is okay." Max buried her face into my neck and pulled me into a tighter embrace. We stood in the hallway holding each other for a few minutes until Max was finally able to open the door with the key. Max opened the door, and I took a step inside.

Colby had already taken his shower and was dressed. He had on a bright pink jumpsuit and a pair of high-heeled shoes prancing around. The music was playing, and he started dancing in the kitchen. Max walked over and looked Colby up and down. Max just shook her head at him.

"Colby, What the fuck are you doing?" Max asked.

"I got a HOT date, my dear Max…and if he is as hot as I hope he will be then I will be doing the walk of shame tomorrow morning," Colby replied as he strutted across the kitchen floor.

"Jesus!" Max blurted out. "Come on Sadie. I will get you a towel and show you where to shower."

Max told Colby it was obvious they needed to have a talk about his date and to stay put. Colby just smiled and curtsied.

When I entered the room after my shower, Max and Colby had just finished their talk because as soon as I entered the room, Max jumped up. "My turn to wash up. Colby. Will you pour Sadie a cup of coffee?" she said as she walked down the hall toward the bathroom.

Colby filled the Lesbian Lovers cup up again. He handed it to me and said, "Are you okay, baby girl?"

"I am okay, Colby. Tubing just will not be on my to-do list anytime soon nor in my distant future."

Colby smiled. "Mine neither, baby girl."

We sipped our coffee. Colby started looking at me strangely.

"Is something wrong, Colby?"

"Are you comfy in those clothes?" Colby asked.

"Not really but I didn't bring anything to sleep in."

Colby nearly yanked me off the bar stool pulling me into his room. Colby's room was covered in half-naked guy posters and extremely tidy. He pulled a pair of sweatpants and a t-shirt out and tossed them to me. "Here, baby girl. These should fit, and you will be a lot comfier." Colby pranced out and closed the door behind him.

By the time I came back into the room, Max was sitting at the bar in the kitchen. Her hair was down and still wet from the shower. She was wearing boy boxers and a tank top. She looked over her shoulder when she heard me come in. "Hey, you! You look a lot more comfortable, and I love the cat t-shirt." Max smiled as she wiggled the fat cat on the front of the t-shirt. "*Oooh so sexy!*"

Colby proclaimed that cat shirts were back in style as he grabbed his keys. Colby kissed Max on the cheek and then me as he pranced by. "Y'all two have fun and *Sadie.* I am glad you are okay." He turned with a swing and skipped out the door. "*Chow!!*" he yelled with the door closing behind him.

Max laughed. "He is such a queen. I don't have much to eat. Is a frozen pizza okay, Sadie?"

"That will be fine, Max."

The oven timer went off, and Max pulled a frozen pizza from the oven. "The pizza is not as good as Larry's, but it will do." Max cut the pizza then she poured two glasses of wine. We sat on the couch with the pizza between us. My strawberries and cheese from earlier were long gone.

My nerves were still on edge from my near drowning experience. We were finally alone. My inner voice was in overdrive and filling my head with all sorts of thoughts. Would there be any more questions? Thinking, of course, there would be. I needed to find a way to answer Max's questions so that I would not be telling her a lie, but I couldn't let her find out about the hell I was living in.

I finished the first glass of wine in two gulps. My eyes were closing as the last drip of wine entered my mouth. When I opened my eyes, all I could see was Max smiling at me.

Max grabbed my glass and refilled it as she asked, "Are you nervous?"

"Sorry… No, just thirsty. That is not true. I am very nervous, Max."

Max gave me a smile. "Don't be Sadie."

"So, tell me about yourself, Sadie. How old are you?"

"twenty-nine for a while longer. How old are you Max?"

"Thirty-one."

"Where do you work, Sadie?"

"At the law office on Fourth," I hesitantly replied hoping and praying the questions would end.

"Fourth Avenue?" I could tell Max was thinking while sipping the wine. "Oh my God! You work for the office of Mo Mahoney the ambulance chaser. That guy is so phony that we call him Phony Mahoney!" Max was laughing. "I am sorry. I know it is just a job, but Christ! That man's commercial on television…have you seen them? LET MO GET YOU MO MONEY!"

"I know, but it pays my bills for now. My boss is nothing like the commercials make him out to be."

"So, what do you do, Max?" I had to think of something to change the subject and get the focus off me.

"I work at the Otis factory making parts for computers, printers and cameras. Tori and I also do odd jobs for people locally to earn extra money." Max finished the last sip of her wine and placed the glass on the coffee table along with the other empty plates.

"You want dessert, Sadie? I have ice cream."

I shook my head no as I took my last sip of wine.

"Do you want another glass of wine, Sadie?" Max asked as she picked up the wine bottle.

Shaking my head and placing my glass on the coffee table next to hers, I whispered no.

"Are you tired, Sadie? Do you want to lie down since you had a busy day?" Max asked as she leaned forward

"No," softly slipped out once more.

"What do want, Sadie?" Max softly said to me as her fingers wrapped around my wrist. Her thumb was rubbing the top of my hand in a soft caress.

Oh my, I thought the sand was starting to fall.

My eyes were looking down watching Max's fingers roll around my wrist.

"Your eyes are lowered again, Sadie."

Taking a couple of deep breaths, I raised my eyes upward toward her. Rolling my tongue over my lips making them wet, I whispered very softly as I studied her eyes, "I want you to kiss me again."

I could really feel the sand was about to fall.

Max smiled with her lips slightly parted. She leaned into me pushing my hair behind my ears. Max's hand slipped to the back of my neck and grasped it. I could feel her fingers pressing into my skin. I closed my eyes and rolled my neck into her fingers. Max placed my hands on her thighs with my palms down. Her mouth was inches from my ear; I could feel her breath on me. "Ask me again, Sadie?" she breathed into my ear.

My eyes were closed when I whispered back, "I want you to kiss me again Max."

Max's fingers tightened around my neck when she heard those words. Her lips moved over my cheek. Then she placed her mouth over mine, our lips moving over each other and our tongues circling each other. Max's fingers were pressing into my neck, holding my lips onto hers.

Then an uncontrollable moan escaped me and rolled over her lips.

Max shifted her body and moaned as she heard me, "Ah...." Her lips separated from mine and her fingers let go of my neck as she blurted, "Jesus, Sadie!"

"Was that wrong? I am sorry. Max! What did I do?" I said in a panic.

"No, No, Sadie it wasn't wrong. It is your moaning. It... Oh God...it has this effect on me. It is completely right, Sadie. I am not sure you know how right it is."

Max laid back on the couch pulling me on her. "Lay with me, Sadie" My head was nuzzled into her shoulder. She pulled some covers over us. Stroking my hair, she whispered, "Who are you?" That was the last thing I remember. The question was never answered. My body must have been exhausted. I was in a deep sleep before I knew it.

My eyes tried to focus on the clock to see the time. It was 3:00am, and my body was still lying on Max just as it was when I fell asleep. I could tell Max was asleep by her breathing, my body rising and falling with each breath she took. Her hair slightly covering her face, I reached up and moved it away. Her face was so beautiful. Max opened her eyes, smiling. She caught me watching her. Pulling me upward, her lips pressed into mine, soft at first, then her kiss got harder and deeper. She made herself stop to whisper over my lips, "Follow me." Taking me by my wrist, she guided me down the hallway. My heart was pounding, but my feet would not stop. I wanted this. I didn't know why. I just wanted it.

I knew more sand was about to fall.

Max's room was lit by the moonlight coming through the window. Turning around, she pulled me into her embrace. Her mouth kissing over my neck and sucking gently between kisses, her mouth trailing up to my ear, nibbling it gently. Then she whispered, "Sadie, I want you." Max traced her mouth back down my neck whispering over my neck, "Tell me what you want, Sadie!"

Max had my vagina on fire. I wanted to moan but reframed because I just didn't know if it was right. I was afraid she would stop like earlier. I didn't want her to stop. My breathing was heavy. I whispered out, "I am scared. I have never…um…been with a woman. I don't know what—" Max kissed me stopping my words.

"Sadie, tell me what you want," Max asked again, as I felt her loosen the strings on my pants.

"I want you to keep going, Max."

Grasping the back of my neck, Max looked into my eyes saying, "You tell me to stop if you need to."

I shook my head yes. My heart felt like it was about to pound out of my chest. My lips would never say stop. My entire body was needing this, needing and wanting her.

Her mouth covered mine and I felt her fingers slip inside the waistband of my sweatpants. Her mouth moved to my neck sucking gently. She ran her hands around to the back and slipped the pants down just below my butt cheeks. Then her hands cupping my cheeks. I could feel her fingers digging into me. Backing me to the bed, Max laid me down, slipping the sweats slowly off. She stood above me looking down.

My eyes were watching as she slipped off her boxers revealing herself. A small patch of hair covered just enough to keep her vagina hidden. Max's eyes were still on me as she slipped her tank top off. Her areola covered the front of her breast; her nipples were small and hard. Leaning over, her fingers slipped into the top of my panties. My breathing was rapid as I lifted my ass and she slid them slowly off. Her eyes were studying me, with my vagina uncovered.

"Stand up and remove the tee," Max ordered while watching me.

Standing, I squirmed out of the tee awkwardly, dropping it to the floor. My breast was lit by the moonlight. My nipples were larger than hers and hard as the cold air hit them. My hands fell across my breasts covering them. She immediately pulled my arms to my side exposing all of me. Reaching out, she took her fingers and traced a circle slowly around my breast. My eyes closed as I struggled to suppress my moan. Her finger slipped down my belly; then I felt it run over my scar. She stopped to study it. I pulled away and covered it with my hands. I tried to say something, but she pulled back, "Don't pull away." Her arm wrapped around my waist holding me close. She sucked on her finger then rolled the wetness over my nipples. I watched her finger as my nipple stiffened under its touch.

"Lay down, Sadie. I want my mouth on your breast."

Hearing her words, I felt myself release a little, and my vagina tighten. Max's body slid in beside me. Gently grabbing my chin, she pulled my face toward her. "You okay. Sadie?"

I shook my head yes since I was unable to speak. My body was showing how tense I really was and I knew Max could tell.

Max continually kept kissing me softly then whispering over my lips she said, "Sadie, close your eyes and breathe." Max's mouth traveled down my neck kissing it in little pecks. Her tongue was just sliding over my skin. Her hand was on my breasts and lifting them ever so gently. Max pulled on my nipples lightly pinching them. Then I felt wetness over them; Max was licking and sucking all around my nipples. Oh, her mouth was on me. I wanted to moan, but I held it back. I was feeling so damn good. My body started to twist under Max's body, and juices were oozing out of my vagina. Max's hand traveled down my thighs as she spread my legs. My breaths were getting harder and deeper with my chest rising. Her mouth was sucking my hard-as-nails nipples as she was grinding on me.

The sand was starting to fall, and it felt SOOO damned good.

I could feel Max's body with every breath. Then, Max started sucking harder, and her own breathing was getting deeper. She was getting excited. Her hand moved down and laid on top of my vagina. Max whispered, "Can I touch you?" I was barely able to speak, but I whispered, "Yes," thinking this felt so good, hell yeah, touch me. *DON'T STOP*. Max moved her leg over mine as she spread my vagina farther apart. Then she slipped her index finger down my vagina and started gently rubbing my clit. Max was still pulling my nipples hard with her teeth then releasing them. My body was on fire. She started kissing upward over my body, letting her mouth find mine. Her tongue slipped into my mouth hard. Her fingers were still rubbing circles around and massaging my clit making it so hard. Then the circling would stop and slip up and down slowly.

Oh my, my… The sand was falling, and it felt so good.

"Sadie, you are so wet. I need you to moan."

I am thinking, shit it felt so good. I wanted to do that sooner.

My moan echoed over her lips as a small explosion occurred. Juices were oozing out of my vagina like I never felt or had done before. I had been suppressing my moan for a long a time.

I cried out, "Oh my God! Oh my God!"

Max moaned deep and hard. "Can I go inside you?"

"Oh, yes Max!" My hips started lifting into her.

Her finger parted my vagina, and she filled me with her finger. My body started raising high off the bed into her finger. I am moaning louder with every stroke of her finger. I was so wet, getting wetter every time her finger would slip in and out of my vagina and dipping deep in me. She kept repeating her fingers movements over, over and over again, each time deeper and deeper. I could not believe Max was about to make me cum.

"Max, I have to…" my body arched hard, and my vagina tightened around her finger. My wetness was just flooding out all over her hand. Max buried her finger deep in me. My vagina was clamping down on her. I was peaking.

"That it is, Sadie. Let me feel you cum."

My body fell back to the bed, and little moans were escaping from me. Max was breathing hard and kissing me deeply. She slipped her body on top of me bracing herself with her arms. Her leg pushed the inside of my thigh making one of my legs crooked. She looked down as she laid her vagina on mine, making sure our vaginas were touching. Max moaned aloud when she ground into me.

Max said, "Sadie, pinch my nipples."

Reaching up, I rolled her nipple between my fingers. Max's body was responding. Her nipples started to swell. I am making this woman excited. My touch was arousing her.

"Harder, harder," Max moaned out as she started using my body. Max's butt was moving up and down as she was grinding our vaginas together. It was a slow grind, then a hard grind rubbing thrust. Max's eyes were closed with her lips parted slightly.

I felt Max's juices run all over my vagina. Max was groaning hard, so I lifted into her. Her nipples were red and swollen from the pinching. I just wanted to wrap my lips around the big red swollen nipples and suck. I lifted my face and put my wet lips around those red swollen nipples and started sucking. Oh no! Max was going to make me explode again.

I moaned over Max's hard nipples, "I'm cumming again!"

Max dug her vagina deeper into mine. Thrusting harder and harder, Max released a loud moan, which made me explode again. Max followed my climax with her own. "Oh yes! Oh yes, Sadie!" Max arched and released her juices all over my vagina. Max's whole body was tensing as she climaxed hard. She collapsed on me, and we were gasping for air as our climaxes ended together. Max moaned softly in my ear as I could tell her last juices were oozing out. Max's lips found mine, and she kissed me passionately.

"That felt so good, Sadie." She breathed over my lips.

Max raised her body over mine, positioning me on my side with my knees bent. She spooned in behind me wrapping her arms around me. We just laid there in silence with her holding me tight for the longest time, listening to each other breathe.

"Max!"

"Yes, Sadie!"

"That is the first time…"

Max cut across me. "I know the first time with a woman."

I said, "No Max! The first time…"

Max cut me off again, and she popped her head up, "The first time you climaxed?

"Yes… no… I mean yes, the first time another person made me climax."

"Really, Sadie? Was it good, Sadie? Are you okay?"

"Oh yes, Max!" I replied. "Did I do okay Max?"

"Dream about my moans, and you will have your answer, Sadie."

Max pulled the covers up and wrapped us up. She kissed the back of my neck.

"It has been a long time since I have been with anyone. Get some rest. Night, Sadie!"

"Night, Max!"

4

"It took all of us to get you back after
the last relationship."
—Tori

It was morning, and my body was waking up slowly. As I stretched my body in the bed, I rolled over to Max, and she was talking on the phone. Max smiled and pulled me over closer to her. I moved over and snuggled into Max's arms. She smelled so good. She felt so good. Max stroked my hair as she talked. With my eyes closed, I enjoyed her touch.

"Tori, listen, I know we are late. Call Mrs. Preakness and tell her we got held up and we will be there by 2:00 pm."

Oh MY, my inner voice said when I realized who Max was talking about—my landlord, Ms. Preakness. Now my thoughts were really going crazy. Mrs. Preakness? Oh no, Max was going over to the place where I stayed and would find out that I live in a boarding house. In my mind, I am debating should I tell her or wait? I was confused and didn't know what to do.

Max told Tori she would pick her up by 1:00pm to go pick up the parts from the hardware store to complete the job. Max then hung up the phone.

"Sleep okay?" Max asked as she rubbed my back.

"Yes. Better than I have for a long time."

I told Max I should be getting ready to go so she could go to work. Max said she had two hours until she needed to leave for work. "Can you please stay?" She pulled me back toward her.

Once again, Max's lips found mine, and she used her body to push me backward on the bed. Pulling away, Max looked down at me smiling with those parted lips. I reached up and traced her lips with my finger. Her mouth engulfed my finger and softly sucked on it.

Oh no, the sand was starting to fall again.

With each suck, I could feel my vagina waking up again. I watched the finger as it slipped in and out slowly. Max whispered, "You had me so turned on last night."

"I have never felt what I felt last night, Max. You were my first."

Max propped up on her elbow hovering over me. She pulled the sheet down exposing my breast then my tummy. Max laid her hand on my scar; I grabbed her hand trying to push it away. I tried to roll over, but Max wasn't letting me. She wrapped her leg around mine under the sheet. Max said, "Stop Sadie! Didn't I tell you not to pull away from me?" I threw my arm over my eyes covering my face. Max leaned over nudging my arm away with her face. "We don't need to talk about it right now." Then she kissed me softly.

It was my past, and that was where it needed to stay. I rolled over and buried my face in her neck. Max held me tight. My body heaved, and the tears started to roll down my cheeks. My past has started to overwhelm my thoughts again, and I didn't want to lie to her.

"Shhh, Sadie! It is going to be okay," Max said. She rocked me until my tears finally slowed and came to a stop.

Finally, I could calm down.

As I wiped my eyes, I asked Max if I could take a shower before I left since I had some errands to do. It would be closer to leave from there and take care of them. In my mind, I was thinking the truth was I wouldn't be able to go back to my room because she would be working there.

Max started pulling my face upward with her finger. She looked me in the eyes, "I am hoping that we could take a shower together."

"I would like that," I whispered softly.

Oh my, the sand was really starting to fall.

The water was slipping along the curves of our bodies as we embrace each other tightly. We enjoyed the warm water rushing over us. Max leaned back letting me lather her hair. She had so much hair, and it was heavy when it was wet. "How long have you been growing your hair?"

"A long time. I have been thinking about letting Zena cut it. It can be a pain to manage sometimes."

I rolled my hands down her back letting my nails rack over her skin. Max shifted as my arms went around her and cradled her breast. Max slowly turned around to face me with water drops sliding down her body. Her body really turned me on. She leaned me back against the wall, and I noticed her breathing had changed.

"Max, don't push me too hard against the wall. It freaks me out."

"Okay, Sadie. I want to hear you cum again." She placed my hands on her breast, and I pinched down on her nipples. Her mouth buried into my neck and she started to suck. Her moaning was muffled and deep.

"Sadie, tell me what you want."

"I want you inside me, Max,"

Groaning into my neck, Max opened my legs, and her finger dug hard into my vagina. "Put your hands above your head." She pinned my wrist to the wall with her free hand. "This okay, Sadie?" I gasped and moaned out. "*Yes!*" It felt so damned good. I couldn't believe she was fucking me good and hard with her finger, slipping to the edge then jamming it hard back into me, over and over. Every time I moaned out, she went harder and faster. My moans were getting louder with every thrust of her finger. Her moans were intensifying with every one of my moans. She reached up grabbing the shower head, both my hands laying on her breast softly twisting her nipples. They were hard and stiff, much harder than the night before. Max's body reacted again to my touch. I heard her mumble "*Sadie*" in my neck before sucking harder on it. She switched to a powerful spray and then it was between our vaginas. Our clits were swelling as the warm water pounded over them. She started to thrust her ass and moaned deeper and deeper. My vagina was about to explode again.

The sand was falling, and this felt so good.

I moaned out, MAX!

Max moaned out, SADIE!

We started to cum together hard and loudly. My vagina was tight. Oh God, I was so tight. My hands grabbed Max's ass as it thrust into me. Our hard nipples were against each other. Max was still sucking hard on my neck. Our moans were mixing as our bodies were rubbing together. Our vaginas exploded, juices rolling down our legs. Our thrusting started to slow, and our breathing was still heavy. We both groaned the same word at the same time "Jesus." We were barely able to hold each other up.

We only had the strength to wrap towels around us and make it to the bed. Falling on the bed, we both were done. There was about an hour left before Max had to meet Tori. I was enjoying this time and didn't want things to end. Eventually, I raised up on my elbow and looked down at Max. Smiling down at her, I leaned over and kissed her gently, her hair smelling of rose petals and skin of baby powder, the two scents teasing my nose. My hand unwrapped her towel. She laid there naked. She let me study her body. Her nipples were no longer swollen. Her hair was trimmed around her vagina. Her mound was tiny and curved hiding her lady's folds. I was laying my hand on her stomach doing circles around her belly button. This woman was so hot.

I told Max she had a sexy belly button. My finger traced downward. Max's eyes closed and she breathed in, and her body tensed up. She grabbed my wrist and stopped it from moving any farther.

"You can't touch me there yet." I could hear the fear in Max's voice. I wasn't going to press her because obviously she also has a past. My hand laid softly on her stomach with my finger circling her belly button again slowly.

"Thanks for an amazing weekend, Max."

"Yes, it was." Max grabbed my hand bringing it to her lips, kissing my knuckles gently.

We finally had to get up and get dressed. We could have laid around all day with each other. For the first time in almost forty-eight hours, I barely thought about the hell in my life.

As I was fixing my hair in the mirror, I had to take a second look.

"OH MY GOD, MAX!" I screamed.

Max ran over from the closet where she was putting on a pair of jeans.

"What is the matter," she asked coming across the room.

"What the hell did you do to my neck?"

I turned my head and pulled back my hair revealing the largest hickey that I have ever seen. The hickey was already turning a dark shade of purple.

Max looked in the mirror at the oddly-shaped rounding purple mark. She wrapped her arms around me from behind, then kissed the hickey softly. Laying her chin on my collarbone looking at me in the mirror, she whispered in my ear; "Sorry Baby, I just got lost in the moment. I just got lost in you." Max kissed my neck softly again. Max stuck out her pouty lip. "Come with me to dinner later?"

"Don't you have a job to get too and yes, I will meet you later." I smiled as I reached up and pushed her pouty lip back in.

Facing each other with the sunlight coming through the window, Max finished zipping her jeans leaving the top button undone as before. I looked down slipping my finger into the open button of her jeans, pulling her toward me, "Do you know how sexy this is?" I asked Max.

Max's eyes lowered to watch my finger as it dipped into the jeans. Looking up, she cupped my face. "Do you know how sexy you are?" Max replied as she pulled me into a kiss. Our lips slowly separated as Max's hand wrapped around my wrist. She led me out of the bedroom and down the hallway and through the living room.

Reaching the door, I heard Colby call out from the couch where he was lying.

"I am not the only one doing the walk of shame this morning!"

Max looked at me and smiled closing the door behind us.

Max kissed me one more time before she closed the car door. "Bye Sadie," she mouthed through the window.

Tori and Lacey were on the front porch as Max pulled her car into the driveway. "Morning guys!" Max spoke out as she approached. Max slapped Tori's hand and leaned over kissing Lacey on the cheek.

"Afternoon!" Lacey said as she grabbed Max. Lacey pulled Max closer and inhaled deeply. "Is that the new smell of Sadie?

"Lacey!" Tori yelled out.

Max just smiled and turned to Tori ignoring the question. Max told Tori they would have to take her truck since they needed to pick up the new water heater for Mrs. Preakness house.

"You want to come, Lacey?" Tori asked knowing hard labor was not Lacey's thing.

"No. Zena is picking me up, and we are going shopping," Lacey replied

"Great! I make the money, and you spend it," Tori leaned over and kissed Lacey softly. "Bye babe."

Max jumped in Tori's truck. They were headed to A. J. Hardware Store.

A.J. Hardware was crowded for a Sunday, but that was to be expected since the next hardware store was in the next city over. Max and Tori looked around the store for a while as they waited for the water heater. Max was looking in a box of clearance items when Tori walked up.

"So, what happened after the excitement yesterday at Hunter's Canyon?" Tori asked.

"We went back to my place, and we got close. Really close, Tori!"

Tori gave Max a smile. "You okay Max? I don't want you to let yourself go back down that old road like the last time."

"I am okay."

"It took all of us to get you back after the last relationship. We almost lost you, and I don't want you to hurt that bad again. You mean too much to all of us" Tori said.

Max quietly said, "Most of you but not all." Max fumbled with some piping in the box.

Tori placed her hand on Max's shoulder. "No Max, even to her you still mean something. Just be careful and remember I am here if you need to talk. Don't keep it inside like the last time and let it eat away at you."

Over the loudspeaker, customer service called their number for the water heater pickup.

"That's us" Max called out as she started to walk away.

Tori pulled Max back. "Max, I am serious."

Max took a deep breath, "I am better now. I am in a better place. I owe that to you, Lacey and Colby. It won't happen again, Tori. I promise. Now Tori, can we get going since we have work to do?"

Tori's facial expressions showed that she was worried about Max as she followed her down the aisle. "Really close, huh? Sadie has that librarian sex appeal, Max. Was the sex hot?" Tori gave Max a cheesy grin when Max turned to give Tori a glance.

Max stopped in her tracks. "I am not sure who is worse, you, Lacey or Colby. And yes, my dear friend Tori, it was on fire." Max returned Tori's cheesy smile before she continues walking down the aisle.

I could not believe I was already missing Max, but I decided to use this free time to get gas and run by the library. I really enjoyed reading books because they keep my mind busy. Books had become my escape from the real world for almost a year now. After the night before I had plenty of thoughts on my mind to help keep my brain occupied. Driving into the gas station, I looked across the street at the shopping center where Larry's Pizza House was. Turning off the engine, I just sat there for a moment and smiled and thought about that night. I would never go out to dinner with a group of strangers, but there was something about Max. She was a magnet, and I was drawn to her. Entering the store, I went down the back aisle looking at the chips. Then I felt a bump from behind pushing me forward a bit.

"How is the water?" this lady whispered as she bumped me.

It was a tall, slim glass-shaped lady. Jesus, it was Zena. I was so busy with my thoughts that I didn't even notice the red sports car parked on the side of the building.

I looked up annoyed. In a sarcastic tone, I replied, "The water is so damn nice."

The words caused Zena's face to go red. Zena started to push me down the aisle into a hallway near the bathrooms. She shoved me against the wall, pressing her body against mine hard, and her hand around my neck. "You bitch." Zena was much larger than I was and could choke me out with ease. Zena turned my head sideways revealing the large hickey. For a moment, Zena's shoulders dropped in defeat. Then Zena's rage took over again. She started to tighten her fingers harder around my neck.

I gurgled out, "Zena, stop. I can't breathe." Her hands tightened.

Just then, Lacey walked out of the bathroom. "Zena, what the hell? Let Sadie go!" Lacey started pulling at Zena's shoulder but wasn't having much luck getting her off me. Lacey yelled and told Zena to stop again. "This will be it, Z. Max will break all ties with you if you hurt Sadie. Max will never forgive you. Z, LET HER GO NOW!"

Lacey and all their friends called Zena "Z" instead of saying her name. Lacey was pleading with Z to let me go. Zena finally released the grip around my neck, but I was still against the wall.

"Let me off this wall," I gurgled out.

Lacey just looked at Z. Lacey mouthed the words, "It is OKAY. Let Sadie go!"

Zena looked at me, released my arm and ran out of the store. My body just slipped down the wall to the ground. I started inhaling trying to replace the air in my lungs that Zena had just pushed out. Lacey helped me get back up. Lacey moved my head side to side looking for damage. Then she ran her fingers over the large hickey before she asked if I was okay.

I tried to steady myself, and I mumbled, "I think so. What did I do to Zena?"

"That's not my story to tell you. You need to talk to Max about that."

I was confused and did not know what was going on. So now my thoughts were running wild again. Lacey apologized for Zena and said her temper could get out of control at times. "You just need to talk to Max because she has all your answers." Lacey said she had to go, and walked away.

I just leaned on the wall, whispering, "Christ! What the hell have I got myself in?"

Outside, Zena was in her car crying when Lacey got in. "Are you all right Z?" Lacey asked as she shut the car door.

Barking out, Zena said "NO! Who the hell does Sadie think she is? Did you see that big ass hickey, Lacey?"

Lacey replied, "Yes, I saw it. Z you must let Max go. Max needs to move on. You need to move on. Your relationship with her isn't healthy. You know we almost lost her." Lacey laid her hand on Z's shoulder as she started to cry again. "Go ahead and cry it out Z. You will feel better."

I paid for the gas and slipped out quickly across the parking lot to the gas pumps. I could see Zena's red sports car out of the corner of my eye. It appeared Lacey was trying to talk to Zena. I knew Lacey would tell Tori about this, which made it almost impossible for me not to tell Max. My mind started to race again, and I had to think about how to tell Max about the assault on me by tall glass. Worst of all, I had to find a way to ask Max about her and Zena.

5

"I didn't want to ask but if you and Zena are a couple I need to know."
—Sadie

Lost in thoughts at the library, time has flown past. The books I selected to read had become extremely addicting. It was not the normal stuff I indulged in, but I had wandered into the romance section, maybe because I had romance on my mind.

When I looked up, it was already 5:00 pm. I needed to go by the house and change my clothes before I went back over to Max's house. But first I had to make sure Max was nowhere near Mrs. Preakness house. The last thing I wanted to explain was why I lived in a boarding room. It had already surprised me that Max never asked where I lived. I guess maybe she had other things on her mind the night before.

I grinned thinking about the things I did the night before. Then my grin widened as I thought maybe tonight would be even hotter than last night.

So, I crept down the street like a stalker. I was trying to get a glance at the cars to make sure I did not see Max's car or Tori's truck. Thank God, they were nowhere in sight. Running in and throwing on a pair of jeans with a hoodie I headed over to pick up Max.

❧

It was around six before I arrived. Max and Colby were outside looking under Colby's SUV hood.

Walking up behind, I said, "Hey Colby, is it okay?" In his flirty tone, Colby said, "Hey baby girl, cute outfit." Since I could not stop smiling, I said thanks and asked him how his date went the night before. Smiling and twirling, Colby responded, "It was wonderful! And how was your evening?" Colby pointed to his neck where the hickey was on my neck. Smiling from ear to ear, I leaned toward him and whispered, "Hot!" Waving his hands, he laughed. Max chimed in from under the hood, "I heard that."

Max was under the car repairing something. Max blurted out, "There you go, Colby. It should be fine now. If not, you are just going to have to break down and order that part. The part I told you to get a month ago."

Colby jumped in the SUV and said, "I know. I know, Max. Thanks." Colby waved his hand and pulled off driving past a blue van.

Max turned wrapping me in her arms. "Hungry?"

"Starving," I whispered in her ear.

I drove us out to a hamburger joint near the canyon called Big Daddy's Burgers. It was a cute place, but there was no inside dining. Instead, the place had picnic tables down a hill near the water. Getting out of the car, Max walked around. Opening my door, she held her hand out for mine. Families and couples were at the picnic tables eating dinner, and I was hesitant about holding hands with Max. Max was patient. Finally, I grabbed her hand. Max smiled as she wrapped her fingers tightly around mine, then pulled me from the car. Max walked in front of me through the tables and up to the window.

Hamburger or hot dog, Sadie? Max asked.

"It doesn't matter to me. I will have what you have."

The cashier behind the window smiled at Max. The cashier leaned over toward the window with her breast almost popping out of her uniform shirt. She said, "Hey Max! Long time no sees. I still need to cash that raincheck." She reached out and ran her index finger down Max's arm.

Max replied, "Hey Cherry, just been busy."

I tried to step away, but Max tightened her grip on me not letting go.

So, Max placed the food order. Two hamburgers all the way, one large fry, and one large onion ring. Max looked at me and asked if diet soda would be fine. I shook my head yes. Max completed the order with two diet sodas.

As Max waited for her change, I told her I would be right back. I needed to go to the restroom. Walking around to the back of the building, I pushed the door open to the restroom. There was one other lady in there washing her hands. Stepping past the lady, I slipped into the stall.

Quickly finishing my business, I exited the stall messing with the buttons on my jeans. I noticed the lady was still in the restroom.

The lady stepped close to me. "You should be ashamed of yourself. It is not right for you to lay with a woman."

I tried to get around the lady at the sink, "I am sorry ma'am. I don't think I know you."

"You have to answer to him," she said.

"Him, who is him?"

"You know him," the lady paused. "God."

As the lady walked toward the door, she mumbled, "You don't know me, but I know you."

What the hell! I said to myself leaning on the sink as I watched the door close.

After getting my thoughts together, I left the restroom. Max had the food and was waiting for me when I came around the corner. As Max handed me the tray, she asked was everything okay, since she saw my face was flushed.

"I'm fine, just some weird lady in the restroom, but she is gone now," I said as I looked around for the lady.

Max asked if the lady was hitting on me. "If so, I will take care of her," Max said as she looked around.

"No, none of that is needed. The lady was just odd." With a smirk on my face, I said, "Was the waitress hitting on you? Do I need to take care of Cherry"?

With a grin on her face, Max said, "Funny, Sadie! Come on, let's eat. I am starving now."

Max took my hand, and we eased our way down the steep hill leading to the picnic tables, holding hands and doing a balancing act with the food tray. The area was lit with white Christmas lights. The water could be heard in the background rushing through the canyon. One family was eating so we picked a table far away from them. The mom seemed to be yelling more at the kids than eating. Max sat beside me with our backs to the family. The headlights of the parking cars at the top of the hill would shine on us every now and then as people would come and go. We shared the fries and onion rings, taking the time to feed each other every so often.

We both made small talk about our day. Max told me about how she and Tori replaced a lady's water heater. Then, I told her about all the books I found at the library. We laughed at the size of the hickey on my neck. The conversation was light and felt natural. We finished the last bite. I knew it was time to talk to her about Zena. I really didn't want to, but if I didn't, I knew Tori would. I was sure Lacey couldn't wait to get home and tell Tori the story how Zena kicked my ass.

Taking Max's hand into mine, I played with her fingers. In my mind, I was trying to figure out how to ask her about Zena. Max lifted my head and held my chin with her thumb and index finger.

Holding my chin, she said, "Something is the matter. Talk to me, Sadie."

Shit, how did she know that? Taking a deep breath, I pulled Max's hand away from my face, wrapping my fingers around hers and laying our hands on my lap.

"Something happened today to me after I left you this afternoon. I ran into Zena at the gas station on Fourth Street, and words were exchanged between the two of us. Things also got a little physical."

Jerking her hands away, Max balled up her fist. Her whole body went ridged. Anger took over the cheerful look on her face. This was the first time I had seen this side of Max. I had seen this type of anger, and I really did not want to see it again.

"What did Zena say and do? Tell ME!" Max slammed her hand down on the picnic table. The food trays bounced up and spilled food over the table.

I jumped because the physical anger scared me. Seeing the outrage in Max's eyes brought back the thoughts of the hell I had just left behind, the hell I was trying to escape—ten years of hell to be exact. I was thinking she couldn't be like him.

I asked Max to turn her body toward me. I threw my leg over Max and slipped in as close as I could. Max enjoyed my body, so maybe my body would keep her calm. Only inches from each other, I tried to umbel Max's fist, placing her hands around my waist. I noticed we were finally alone at the tables. The mom at the other table had dragged the kids away kicking and screaming up the hill. Reaching behind my back, I undid my bra, releasing my breast under the hoodie. I took Max's hands and slipped them under the hoodie placing them on my bare breast.

"What are you doing, Sadie?"

I told Max, this was how we were going to talk, just like this, as I wrapped my arms around her neck.

Max cupped my breasts and leaned into me. Her shoulders were starting to relax, and the tension was starting to release. She took a deep breath. "What happened, Sadie?" Max asked as she was kneading my breasts softly.

I started to explain what happened, how Zena saw me at the gas station and then pushed me against the wall. I think she was upset when she saw the hickey and knew that we had been together. Then Zena started to choke me. Max started to tighten her hold, and her fingers squeezed my breasts harder as she listened. I adjusted Max's grip as I continued to explain what had happened, how Lacey was there and talked Zena down until she let me go. I asked Lacey why Zena was so mad at me, how Lacey told me it wasn't her story to tell and Max would have to answer my questions because it was her story.

"So, I need to know Max, what is going on? I didn't want to ask but if you and Zena are a couple I need to know."

"NO! NO! We are not!" Max quickly answered. Max tried to

pull her hand off the soft breast, but I slipped my hand under the hoodie and pressed her hand back on my breast.

"Leave your hand there. It calms you. Just tell me the story, Max."

Max explained they were together at one time but it was complicated, and it didn't last.

Max took a deep breath. "Zena does not want me, but she doesn't want me to be with anyone. Sadie! I promise you we are over. I am not that type of girl. You are my first after Zena, and it has been a year since we broke up. We try to be friends, but it is hard at times."

Max inhaled then exhaled for the longest time "If she hurt you, Sadie, I swear…"

I placed a finger over Max's mouth stopping her words. Kissing Max tenderly, I told her how I really liked her and most important I believed her. I explained how deep down I knew she and Zena were not together but couldn't figure out why Zena was so angry at me.

"I also need to tell you something since we are being open with each other. The house that you went to today to replace the water heater, I rent a room from Mrs. Preakness. I was afraid and embarrassed to tell you. I know it is not the best place to live, but it is affordable."

"None of that stuff makes a difference to me, Sadie."

The Christmas lights turned off, and we were now overwhelmed by the pitch-black darkness of the night.

I whispered in Max's ear," Now, ask me what I want?"

Max breathed out, "What do you want, Sadie?"

I leaned into Max's ear and whispered, "Make me climax without taking my clothes off. Make me cum here in the dark on this picnic table."

Max became excited and pressed her lips hard to mine. Max rolled my nipples between her fingers. She told me to moan. Max watched as I released a long deep moan. Max pulled the hoodie up, resting it on top of my breast. Max ordered me to put my arms behind my back. Pulling her belt from the loops, she tied my arms behind my back. I felt the tug on the belt. She told me she was going to suck my nipples until I begged her to stop.

The sand was starting to fall a little more.

I moaned "Max" as my vagina cramped.

Max buried her face in my chest. I wiggled as I watched Max's tongue trace my right nipple, groaning as I watched her tongue lick over to the left nipple then circle it.

"I love sucking these nipples," Max moaned over my stiffening nipples.

I was trying to pull my hands free but was unable.

With a mouthful of my swollen nipple, Max mumbled, "Don't pull away." Max was sucking hard on my right nipple. The sucking was a little painful, but it was feeling so damned good. Pulling it out with her teeth then sucking back in fast, over and over again, both hands pushed my breast up, her mouth sucking on one nipple as her finger twisted the other causing pain and pleasure to shoot through my body.

Moaning harder, I called out, "OOOOH, Max!" I think Max could tell I was not at my limit yet. When I moaned out, she clamped down harder. My right nipple was bright red and hard as hell. I could feel it throbbing. Max latched down on the left nipple, her teeth racking over it as she sucked it harder and faster. Max pulled away for a moment; she looked up into my eyes as her tongue rolled over my nipple.

"Ah…"

Oh my, this sand was really starting to fall.

Max was breathing hard while rubbing her body against mine. I just knew her vagina was on fire because of the pleasure I was feeling. Using one of her hands, Max pulled her shirt up and then the sports bra over. Her nipples became erect as soon as the cool night air hit them.

Moaning out in pleasure, I said, "Max please!"

Max reached behind me releasing the belt and then pulled me down on top of her. Her hand guided my mouth to her breast.

"Suck my nipples," Max echoed out. "Use my body to please yourself. Go ahead and fuck me."

Max was holding my head down, and I was sucking her hard nipples. I was moaning as I was rippling over the nipples. Now, Max had both her hands on my ass helping our vaginas grind together through our jeans.

Max couldn't hold out anymore. Hearing me moan as I was being pleasured, it was too much for her to handle. "I need to cum. Oh, Sadie, I can't stop…."

Max thrust up exploding under me. Her body was twisting and moan after moan was escaping with every breath. With every explosion, Max's body was arching and pushing into mine. I then released her nipple out of my mouth.

Suddenly, I screamed out, "Yes that's it!" I arched and started to cum, several times, juices flowing with every spasm. We both collapsed gasping. The only thing we could do was just lie there allowing after climax explosions to occur.

The sand was falling.

Max wrapped her arms around me and whispered, "I like you too, Sadie."

Sitting up, Max wrapped her arms around me helping me button my bra. I helped pull Max's bra and shirt back down. Our lips found each other in the dark, and we kissed each other tenderly, holding hands sweetly in the night, our fingers playing just like our bodies just did.

Max told me she had to go back to work at the factory the next day. She was going to be on a twelve-hour shift with mandatory overtime, which meant I might not be able to see her as much. Max worked from eight in the morning till eight at night, and with the overtime, it would probably be more like eight till ten.

"That is a lot of hours, and I know you will be exhausted."

"It is only for four days, Sadie. I am used to it. Next Friday is my last softball game at 5:00 pm. There will be a party at Tori and Lacey's house after the game. So, Sadie, will you come with me to the game and the party? Please?"

I just must ask, "Will Zena be there?"

Max lowered her head, "I promise! Zena will not be saying anything else to you again. I will be making sure of that. Please don't let her stop us from being together and happy."

"Max, please don't do anything. I can handle it."

"Sadie, you shouldn't have to handle anything. I just need for you to know she and I are no more. We are over."

"I trust you, Max. I haven't been this happy in a very long time. I have only been with one person before you in my whole life. I don't know how this is supposed to go," I said as I kissed Max softly.

"Only one? And you just fucked me like that?" Max asked curiously.

"I read a lot. Max, you are the only one that has made me climax like that. The man I was with, just fucked me for years and years and years…" I said in a voice that seemed to start to trail off as I started to stare into space. It was like I was in a trance. Then a tear rolled down my cheek.

"Sadie! Hey Sadie?" Max said lightly while shaking me. Max was trying to get me to come back. She could not figure out where I went, but she knew it must have been a dark, awful place because I had shut down.

"Sadie? Talk to me."

Aloud, I screamed, "NO! DON'T!" as I pulled away from Max almost falling off the bench. Max caught me and pulled me back wrapping her arms around me tightly.

"What the hell did that man do to you, Sadie?"

I just quietly sat in Max's arms becoming wrapped up in her and the darkness, my inner voice saying, you don't want to know, Max, what he did to me. It was best that Max never found out.

Headlights appeared at the top of the hill near the parking lot. There was a shining bright light blinding us. The lights kept going from low to high beam. We covered our eyes to protect them from the brightness.

"Who is that? Do you think it is a cop, Max?"

"That's no damn cop, and it better not be Zena either." Max angrily answered as she started to get up. So, I pulled Max's arm and told her not to go.

The lights slowly started to roll backward. The brightness was swallowed up in the night. Once again, we were consumed with darkness.

"See, they are gone, Max."

Ring, Ring Max's phone sounded.

"Yes Tori, it's late. What's the matter?" Max's eyes never left the hill. "I am on my way."

Max said we needed to go now as she grabbed my hand and headed up the hill. "Colby is in the emergency room."

6

"Max! I am sorry. I don't know why I
did it."

—Zena

The hospital was on the other side of town. The drive was almost twenty minutes, and few words were spoken between us. I could tell Max's thoughts were consumed about Colby. The only thing Tori said was Colby had been attacked, and the ambulance was taking him to Pulse General Hospital. Max's phone lit up the inside of the car with every text she was receiving.

As I pulled into the emergency room parking lot, I could barely get the car stopped before Max tried to get out. She walked around the car to my side and opened the door. "Come on," holding her hand out for me to place my wrist in her hand.

I asked Max if she wanted me to come in with her and if she didn't, I would understand. Max reached down, grabbed my wrist and pulled me out of the seat. My feet were doing double steps trying to keep up with her pace. Max rushed to the front desk barking at the poor lady up front. "Where is my friend? Take me to him!" The lady looked up startled dropping a stack of papers. Wrapping my hand around Max's upper arm to try to calm her down, I stepped forward.

"Ma'am we are looking for Colby."

I turned to Max. "What is Colby's last name, Max?"

"Dodson," Max replied.

Turning back to the still startled lady, "We are looking for Colby Dodson. He was brought in by the ambulance."

The lady behind the desk fumbled through papers. I could tell Max was becoming more and more impatient. She was starting to rock from side to side. I squeezed her upper arm and mouthed "Relax" to her.

The front desk lady said Colby was still being evaluated so we could wait in the waiting room. She told us to sign in with our name and address on this clipboard. The lady pointed and said to go through those doors, and it would be the third door on the left. When we went to step away, the lady called us back. Screaming, "Here are your passes," waving the passes in the air wildly.

I just grabbed the passes and Max grabbed my wrist pulling me toward the double doors. When the doors opened, we saw Tori and Lacey in the hallway. Tori was pacing back and forth like a caged animal.

"What happened, Tori?" Max asked as we approached her.

Tori stopped pacing. "All we know is that Colby was found behind the bank. It appeared he was at the ATM when he was attacked. A lady saw his shoe in the alley and went to investigate. He was unconscious, so she called 911. I could only get a glance of him before they rolled him in from the ambulance. His face was covered in blood. It looked bad, and he was unconscious. It was scary, Max."

Lacey rubbed Tori's back softly. "He will be fine."

"Was he robbed?" Max asked.

"We don't think so, Max," Lacey answered.

Max let go of my wrist. She leaned against the wall. Max ran her hands through her hair laying her head back as she closed her eyes.

"Max, there is something else," Tori said in a different tone.

Max opened her eyes. "What?"

Tori looked at me then back at Max. She blew a breath out. "Zena is in the waiting room," she mumbled out.

Max jumped off the wall without saying a word. She was heading full force to the waiting room. Tori was on her heels trying to slow Max down. I went to follow Max, but Lacey cut me off.

"Stop!" Lacey ordered. She put both hands on my shoulders.

Lacey planted herself between Max and me. There was no way I could get around her. Out of everyone, Lacey had the rock-solid body. Lacey must have worked out every day because her body was fit and she always looked nice. Her picture was on the for-sale signs all around Pulse. She was ranked one of the best realtors in the area.

"Let's go to the café in the lobby," Lacey said.

Looking over Lacey's shoulder, I could see Max pushing the

door open and then she disappeared quickly.

"Come on. I promise it will be fine. Tori always has Max's back."

Lacey interlocked our arms and started to guide me down the hallway. I glanced in the waiting room as we walked by. Max had Zena pinned in the corner of the waiting room. Zena's arms were folded up in front of her and Max was holding her wrist with both of her hands. I knew that wrist hold anywhere because that was how she held my wrist. Then I started thinking; I thought that wrist hold was just for me. Maybe Max held other women's wrist the same way. Maybe I wasn't special at all.... My feet stopped so I could look, but Lacey pulled me past the door.

Zena was looking at her phone when Max entered the waiting room. Max grabbed the phone throwing it into the chair. Max backed Zena into the corner and grabbed both her wrists. She held them down, and she just stood there looking at her. Max was breathing hard, and the anger was flowing from her. Tori stood in the corner of the room.

"Max! I am sorry. I don't know why I did it." Zena pleaded.

"You did it, Zena, because you are a self-righteous bitch. I don't get it! You destroyed me, and when I start to get a little happiness, you try to fuck things up. You have been flaunting cunt in my face day after day since we broke up."

Max yanked her arms down making Zena winch in pain.

"Don't you ever touch Sadie or even mumble a threatening word to her or about her. If you do, I swear Zena, I will hurt you. You didn't want me. You just threw me away. But now you don't want anyone to have me. Zena, something died that day. It was your control over me," Max angrily told Zena.

"Max, I do want you." Then Z forced her lips to Max's lips.

Max pulled away. Tori stood straight up. She was going to walk over. Max raised her hand to stop her.

"Z, get this shit straight and understand me clearly! I like Sadie. The last forty-eight hours I have been very happy. I have smiled, laughed, cried and fucked good. Zena! I don't want you anymore."

Zena's head dropped, and a tear rolled down her cheek.

Through her tears, Zena mumbled, "I know."

"Don't fuck with Sadie again or we will be done for good." Max let go of Zena's wrist and turned away.

Max started walking past the couch in the lounge when she stopped suddenly. Then suddenly she started to sway before she collapsed on the cushions. Tori ran over catching Max before she hit the floor.

Propping Max up on the couch, Tori asked, "Max! Are you okay? Talk to me!"

"I am fine, Tori."

"Did you take your meds today, Max?" Tori sat down to steady Max.

"I am fine; it was probably just all the stress that got to me," Max mumbled. "Why haven't they come out to talk to us about Colby yet?"

"I'm not sure what is taking them so long," Tori said in a concerned voice.

Zena had taken a few steps closer to Max. "Max, are you okay?" Zena whispered.

"I am fine, Z. Just give me some space."

"I am so sorry, Max," Zena whispered out from a distance.

Tori looked up at Zena. "Back off, for now, Z and let her get herself together," Tori replied.

Lacey and I were sitting in the corner of the café. The lights of the city were illuminating the sky. There was a peaceful look for a moment. Lacey ordered a latte, and I got a hot tea. For the first few minutes, we just sat there sipping our drinks quietly. My mind was on Max and wondering what was happening in the waiting room.

"So," Lacey started talking. "Are you thinking about Max, Sadie?"

"Yeah, I am," I replied while sipping my tea.

"Tori will make sure Max is handling everything. Tori would take a bullet for that girl."

"How long have you and Tori been together?"

"Going on ten years this February seventh. We met when I sold her a house on Brooke Lane. Our relationship took off like a rocket. Things have changed over the years; our fights are doozies at times, and it feels like we are always on the brink of breaking up. But I swear I love that big fool."

"Max invited me to the party at your place Friday," I said suddenly.

"Good. It will be a wild night. Okay Sadie, enough of the small talk. Spill it! By the size of that hickey on your neck, this weekend must have been…how do I say it…enlightening?"

A blush came across my face. "It was exciting, but I am not sure I should talk about it."

"So, I guess I get no details, Sadie, huh?" Lacey sipped on her drink. "That's okay. All I can say is, Max has a lot of friends that care about her. We will make sure she doesn't get hurt by anyone. And that's not a threat; that's just the truth. Sadie, I'm just telling you, just don't hurt Max. When Max commits, she commits hard. Max is a special person."

"I can tell she is very special. I would never hurt Max. Do you think that is what Zena needs to know? Max did tell me she and Zena were together, but it didn't last."

"Okay," Lacey replied.

That was a weird tone in her response; it caused crazy thoughts to go through my mind. I was now wondering if there was something missing that I was not being told.

There was another lady in the café, and she just dumped a tray in the trashcan. I could hear the lady walking, but I could only see the back of her. The lady was now heading to the door when I looked up and got a good glance at her. In my mind, I thought there was something familiar about her. Lacey turned her head to look in the direction that I was looking.

"What's wrong? Is it Max or Tori?" Lacey asked.

"No, it is just something about that lady who had just walked out. I swear I have seen her before at Big Daddy's Burgers."

"A lot of people eat there, Sadie," Lacey said.

"No. This particular lady lectured me in the restroom of the restaurant about being with a woman. It was very uncomfortable and made me feel weird."

"The lady is gone now. Maybe it wasn't her." Lacey was trying to distract me.

"Maybe," I replied, but I still had a very funny feeling about this lady.

Lacey touched my hand, "Let's go see what our girls are doing." We pushed the chairs back and stood up.

"Sadie, just so you know, Z is a best friend of mine but so is Max. Hopefully, we can become friends too. Honestly, I never thought we would see Max happy again, but she seems to be." Lacey smiled softly. "Welcome to our circle, Sadie."

I smiled. "Thanks."

We timed it perfectly. The doctor was walking into the waiting room at the same time we arrived. So, we just followed him in. Max stood up as soon as she saw the doctor come in.

Max leaned over and whispered into Tori's ear, "Not a word to Sadie about me not feeling good." Tori shook her head in agreement. Both Tori and Max gave Zena a look. Zena knew her lips better be sealed for now.

I walked past Tori and slipped my body into Max. Max wrapped her arm around my waist. Zena stood behind us with her head lowered.

The doctor asked if there was a relative here of Colby Dodson. Without hesitation, Max said, "I am." The doctor looked Max up and down then asked to speak to her in private. Max told the doctor to go ahead and talk to her in front of everyone. The doctor looked over the chart.

"Well, Mr. Dodson has a laceration and a concussion. We placed stitches in to close the cut. We will keep him for twenty-four hours to make sure there is nothing else going on. He is waking and should make a full recovery. He also gave the police a statement."

"That's great news, doctor. We are so glad to hear that," Max said with a sense of relief. Max leaned over and kissed my forehead then gave Tori a high five. The doctor gave us a stare when Max kissed my forehead, but I really didn't care. It felt natural. The doctor cleared his throat and asked if anyone has any questions.

"Yes. Can we see Colby?" Max asked.

Yes, as soon as we get him in a room, the doctor replied. Then the doctor left. Zena decided it was best she left before everyone saw Colby. She told Lacey to tell him she would swing by in the morning before she opened the beauty shop.

Zena owned and operated a local beauty salon. She was one of the best hairdressers in town. Customers were on a waiting list to get into her shop. At least, that was the buzz around town. I didn't know because I always saved money and trimmed my own hair.

We entered Colby's room, and it was dark. The only light on in the room was coming from the hotel across the street. Max sat on the side of the bed and wrapped Colby up in the longest hug. She whispered in his ear, "You stupid queen," while tears filled her eyes. Max kissed Colby's temple softly.

Colby whispered, "I will be fine. Lesson learned. Don't go to the ATM machine late."

Tori asked, "What happen, Colby?"

In a weak voice, Colby told us some of the events, but things were still foggy. "All I know is I got my money from the ATM. I remember my phone dinging from a text. It was Charles. He is the man I had a date with last night. We were supposed to be meeting after I got off work for drinks."

Colby laid back in the bed rubbing his head.

Colby worked as a bartender at a local bar. It was called MadJax's Bar and Grill. A lot of gays and lesbians hung out there, but some straight people also went there. The crowd was always a good mix. It was operated by a sister and brother named Maddison and Jaxson. It sat on the outskirts of town.

Colby stopped rubbing his head and continued with the story.

"Next thing I remember was…was waking up here." Colby laid his head back down. "My head is throbbing."

"The doctor said you can probably get released tomorrow. Tori and I will be working twelve-hour shift. Can you pick him up, Lacey?" Max asked.

"I will be in the city handling a sale. I will be home late," Lacey replied.

"I can get him. I get off at four," I spoke up.

Max kissed my hair, "Thanks. Just make sure he gets home."

Thank you, Sadie. We all appreciate it," Tori chimed in.

The nurse walked in. "Time to go, ladies. Let the patient get some rest."

Max kissed Colby on the forehead. "See you tomorrow my queen," she said, pulling him into a tight hug. "You scared me, Colby. I can't imagine my life without you. Who would keep me straight?"

"I love Max. I am safe."

We exited the hospital together, talking about how lucky Colby was and that it could have been a lot worse. It was close to midnight, and I was tired. Poor Max had to get up and go to work a twelve-hour shift. We decided Tori and Lacey would drop off Max because they go right by her apartment complex. I was disappointed that Max and I must separate, but it made no sense to drive Max home. My room was in the opposite direction.

"Hey Sadie, isn't that your gray car over there next to my truck?" Tori asked as we entered the parking lot.

"Shit!" I yelled out. I had a flat tire. Tori and Max changed the tire while Lacey and I stood on the sidelines like cheerleaders. Max was quiet, and I was not sure if it was from her being tired or mad. I knew she thought Zena did this to my tire. Once the tire was changed, Tori and Lacey said their goodbyes to me.

"I will be there in a second," Max told Tori.

Max pulled me close, wrapping her arms around my waist. She leaned over kissing me softly and tenderly. "This weekend has been so amazing," Max whispered over my lips. Placing her forehead on mine, she whispered again, "I wish it didn't have to end."

"Me too Max."

7

"Boss, it is not a male; it is a female."
—Blue van woman

A dark blue van had been parked on the street for about two hours. The night had swallowed it up. The woman in the dark blue van sat staring down the empty street waiting for any sign of life. An empty Big Daddy Burger box sat on the dash along with a half-empty forty-ounce soda in the cup holder. A Pulse General Hospital visitors pass lay crumbled in the seat next to her. The inside of the van was filled with left-over cigarette smoke. Tapping her long nails on the steering wheel, the woman in the blue van was starting to get very agitated waiting. She had been sitting there waiting since she saw the address on the sign-in sheet at the hospital. Suddenly, the dead street had life. A pair of headlights rounded the corner, slowly illuminating the treetops. The woman in the blue van ducked and watched as the headlights pulled into the driveway. The figure of a girl in jeans and a hoodie jumped out, entering the house and disappearing quietly into the night.

The woman fumbled in the dark for a cell phone. She opened the phone and started dialing a New York number. It was about 1:00 am, but that didn't seem to be a concern. A groggy, angry man on the other end of the phone line picked up. He answered quickly from a deep sleep like he had been waiting for the phone call for months.

"Hello!" a deep voice answered the phone.

"It's me," the woman in the blue van answering back. "I found her."

"Where?" the man voice came to life.

"A small town, down in Pulse, Virginia."

The phone went silent.

"Boss?" the blue van woman asked breaking the silence.

"Go ahead and tell me what you know!" the man ordered.

"I haven't found out too much boss other than she is living in a house in town. I'm still trying to find out if she has a job. Not sure if she is using her real name or a fake one yet. But, there is one major thing."

The man angrily barked out, "TELL ME!"

The woman reluctantly said, "She is involved with someone."

The woman could hear clicking on the other end of the phone. When the boss got upset, he would click this fidget thing he carried everywhere. She knew when the clicking started, it wasn't good.

"Who is he?" the man said in a harsh tone.

The woman lit a cigarette nervously. "Boss, it is not a male; it is a female."

Once again, the phone went silent. The silence seemed to last forever. The only sound between the two phones was the click, click, and click, the sound from the fidget.

He finally asked, "Do you have proof of this?"

"Yes. I have pictures of them having sex on a picnic table tonight."

"Send them to me now!" he ordered with his voice filled with rage. "Find out more. I want you to make her nervous. DO YOU UNDERSTAND?"

"Yes, I understand, and I paid a local thug to beat up a friend of hers tonight," the woman answered in a nervous voice.

Good! When I get her back…I swear…I will cage her. She will pay." The man slammed the phone down and hung up.

It was almost 4:00pm, and I was watching the clock tick by slowly. I was leaving work and going straight to the hospital to pick up Colby. I was excited to get back in Max's apartment. My plan was to stay with Colby until Max got home.

The past weekend was all I could think about. My thoughts filled my work day. My mind raced from Max's first touch at the softball game, our first kiss, the feel of her hands on me, the fullness of her fingers inside me and the pain of my swollen nipples. Also, the explosions Max gave me for the first time by just using her hands. Oh my, my, my… Closing my eyes, I could hear Max moaning and hear her loving words. Throughout the day my vagina would be ignited by just the mere thoughts of us together. I could not believe the happiness I felt. My thoughts had me in a daze, and I could barely complete any work.

I was glad Mr. Mahoney was in court all day so he would not see my low productivity. The clock finally clicked over to the hour. I gathered my things quickly, put the lock on the door and headed to my car.

I started the long walk to the roof where my car was parked. I always parked on the rooftop in the parking garage across the street. The roof parking was less crowded plus roof parking was free. The parking garage normally filled up fast during the week. It was really the only available area for parking in the downtown section. Shoppers and employees of the local businesses used the garage.

The garage was old and run down. The family who owned it had moved away from Pulse a long time ago. The family had the realty office where Lacey works collect the fees monthly and send the money to them. The family had never invested in the upkeep of the parking garage.

On my way to the steps that went to the rooftop, I pushed the door open. The door was heavy as hell and made of heavy metal. The door slammed hard *BAM* behind me causing me to jump.

"Geesh" I mumble every time. I hated that damn door.

I started the climb up the three-story building. I figured using the steps would allow me to get in my exercise better than just walking down the ramp where the cars exited. Finally reaching the top of the stairs, out of breath, I tried to push the door with my shoulder. The door did not budge. So again, I tried to push harder using my whole body to pound on the door. The door still didn't open. I tried wiggling the doorknob. The door would not open.

"Hey! Anyone out there, the door is jammed shut!" I screamed in the small crack of the door. Damned old building.

Fussing as I walked back down the steps. I stumbled once

when I took two steps at one time. That made me even more enraged. I tried to push the other door. It just bounced my body back off it.

"Damn it," I mumbled as I tried to push harder.

"HEY, HEY! I am stuck in here. Anyone? Hey!" I yelled as I desperately kept pushing the door.

"HELP!"

Then I noticed a small hole in the door. I could see the street outside through the little hole. The street was bare, no cars, no people.

I sat down on the steps and started to fumble for my cell phone in my purse. Looking down at the phone "NO SERVICE" was running across the screen.

"Shit!"

Now, my mind was wondering what the hell I should do. I thought maybe I would try to send a text, but then I thought who in the hell would see it or would it even work? Max was at work, and I didn't want to bother her. Mr. Mahoney was in court so he would not have his cell phone on. But I guess I could try to send it to him one time if I had service.

So, I tried.

Mr. Mahoney, this is Sadie. I am stuck in the stairway of the parking garage. If you get this message. can you please call someone to open the door? To –Mr. Mahoney

Send

The message said, "Sent Failed."

Damn it! I looked at my watch, and it was 4:30.

Surely, workers would be getting off soon, and someone would open the door. My inner voice popped up and just kept telling me to keep calm.

I jumped up and started pounding on the door.

"HELP! Hey, HELP!" I was panicking and could feel my heart starting to race.

So, I ran up the flight of stairs and slammed my body into the door trying to open it again. The door was still not giving way. So, I ran back down the stairs. My breathing was getting heavy by the time I reached the bottom of the stairs. My body could barely attack the door by this time.

I slumped to the floor gasping for air. I felt like I had no air. There was no air in there!

Being locked in the stairway brought back some very bad memories. My eyes were closed as my mind drifted back to the hell I was living in.

The punch came from nowhere. I was in the kitchen cooking when I heard him come in. I turned to hand him a glass of scotch. Scotch was always his drink of choice. It was a man's drink, so I had heard so many times. Instead of him grabbing hold of the glass his fist contacted my face. The room spun as my body fell to the floor; the glass dropped, shattering into millions of pieces all over the kitchen floor. That image was always stuck in my mind, so much broken glass. My face started to burn as my body laid on the floor below him. He was standing above me yelling.

"You told your sister the truth about what happened to your stomach. You stupid bitch! I give you everything, and this is how you repay me? You want for nothing YOU WHORE!"

He kicked me hard in the shin. I screamed out and pulled into a fetal position.

He grabbed the flour on the counter and threw it over me. The white powder coved my body like a blanket.

Maybe you need to be treated like a whore!

His six feet two inch tall and 240-pound body was pressing my five feet five inches and 130-pounds body into the kitchen floor. He had his nasty tongue in my mouth. With his mouth open, you could tell he already had his scotch. His mouth reeked of it, nasty distinguishing breath. He reached under my dress and ripped my panties into two pieces. His teeth biting on my breast and his hands slipped around my throat. "Keep your ass still!" he ordered.

I had seen a lot of his anger, but this was rage. He has always been verbally abusive, but lately, he has been physically abusive.

"Don't do this!" I pleaded.

"Don't do what? Have sex with my wife?" he said with his nasty smelling mouth.

He undid his pants, and I could feel his dick was already erect. He stroked his old nasty dick a few times.

His veins were popping on his forehead. Now, he was between my legs, and he just jabbed his dick into me. He tore my vagina when he entered. He just pounded me as he always did, hard thrusting until I could hear he about to cum. Then, he would put his dick deeper in me and release cum inside of me. It felt like he was pissing in me. The only thing I could do was just lay there with my eyes closed, hoping and praying he would hurry up and finish.

He stood above me zipping his pants.

He threw the scotch bottle back and took a swig.

I laid on the floor with my dress pulled up above my waist, and my face swelling.

He suddenly grabbed my hair and pulled me across the floor, screaming as my body was dragged along. He stood me up pressing my body against the wall. I couldn't breathe. He was so heavy against me then he threw me in the closet locking the door. I would stay there until morning in the dark, alone, with nothing but my thoughts. That was the night I decided I was going to leave and get the hell out. I just knew I had to get out of that hell before that man killed me.

Suddenly, I popped open my eyes and realized I was still locked in the stairwell. I felt like I had lost time. I wasn't sure if I had fallen asleep or just passed out. It was 5:15 pm by my watch. I reached above my head, wiggled the doorknob and pulled the door. It was still locked.

I pulled myself up and looked out the hole in the door. Suddenly, an eyeball looked back. I jumped back and fell to the floor.

"Fuck!" I screamed.

"Hey! I need help. The door is stuck." I was fighting my way back up to the hole. The eyeball was gone, but I could see a figure of a shadow on the other side.

"Hey, you!" I said desperately.

A very low voice came from the other side. "I don't know you.... Is that what you said?"

"What? I can't hear you?" I called back. "Please get help! The door is jammed."

"Sure," the woman's voice replied.

I watched the shadow walk away.

I ran up the stairs to try to open the roof door. It was still jammed. Once again, I reached for my cell phone. I hit resend on the message to Mahoney. Finally, my phone dinged as the message was delivered.

It went through. I had to laugh.

It was now around 5:30 when I heard banging on the door.

"Sadie, you in there?" It was Mr. Mahoney.

"YES, Yes, Mr. Mahoney, I am in here, and the door is stuck," I screamed back.

"Stand back!" Mr. Mahoney yelled.

It took three body slams against the door before it released, throwing Mahoney almost into the floor as his body flung inside.

"Jesus! That's gonna hurt tomorrow," he moaned.

As soon as the door opened, I ran outside. Leaning over, I tried to catch my breath. I was finally free.

"Are you okay, Sadie? This garage is really old and broken down. I wouldn't use the stairs anymore. Do you want me to drive you home?" Mahoney said in a concerned voice.

"No, Mr. Mahoney. I will be okay but thank you for coming to help me. I have to go now. I am really late to pick up someone." I walked to the car exit ramp. I knew I would be walking this ramp from then on. I might be parking on the first level from then on also. Once safe inside my car, I dialed the hospital.

The operator answered. "Pulse General Hospital. How may I direct your call"?

"Can I be connected to Colby Dodson's room please?"

"Hello," Colby answered.

"Hey, Colby! This is me, Sadie. I got out of work a little late, but I am on my way."

"That's fine Sadie. They are still doing paperwork. When they said twenty-four hours observation, they meant it."

With a sigh of relief, I said, "Okay Colby, I am going to stop by the grocery store and get groceries to make spaghetti for us for dinner."

"That sounds so much better than the food they fed me here today," Colby replied.

"See you soon, Colby."

So now my focus was back on being excited about seeing Max again. I buried deep the thoughts of my wicked past.

I started the car and pulled out slowly. The blue van followed.

8

"Maybe there was a heart in there."
—Sadie

Finally, I arrived at the hospital. Entering the hospital room, the air was filled with a lot of laughter. For just a second, I am hoping it was Max, but as the door flew open, I see the blonde hair. OMG, it was Zena sitting on the side of the bed with Colby.

"Hey, baby girl!"

Colby seemed like his cheerful self again.

"Hi, Colby! Hi Zena." I spoke to her in a mellow tone of voice.

"Still waiting on the last paperwork, Sadie. Shouldn't be too much longer. My stomach has been craving that spaghetti since you mentioned it earlier," Colby stated while snapping his fingers.

Zena stood up and approached me. "We need to talk, Sadie. Can we go out in the hallway?"

I just shook my head yes.

"Colby, we will be right back," Zena blurted out as I followed her out the door.

"Play nice, Zena," Colby yelled back.

We entered the hallway. Zena walked past me. "Come on down to the end. There is a bench we can sit on. My feet are killing me because I have been on them all day." Zena pulled her high heels off and walked barefooted the rest of the way.

Zena was so tall that her legs went on forever. Walking behind her, I noticed her beautiful shape. Her jeans were tight, and she had a perfect round ass. I believed she knew it because she carried herself in such a manner. Zena's confidence spilled out of her.

We sat down, both of us staring out the window. My heart was in my throat. I felt the blood pumping with every thump of my heart. Clearing my throat, I told her I had a hectic day. "Colby and I need to get going soon, so what can I do for you?"

Zena took a deep breath. "I am sorry about the other day. My anger got the best of me. I am sure Max told you about us. It has been hard on me letting her go. But—I know I need to for Max's wellbeing. There was a time when we had the most passionate love. Letting her go doesn't mean I will stop watching out for her. I am going to try to accept you and her as a couple. You understand?"

I looked at Zena for a while and finally saw some feelings in her. Maybe there was a heart in there.

"Well—first, I don't know if we are a couple, but I do like her. Second, I won't hurt Max, so there is nothing to watch as far as that is concerned. Last, I appreciate you trying to accept me and Max being together but, I have a question for you, Zena. Did you flatten my tire last night here?"

"What? NO! I didn't, I swear. I picked up a girl in the café. She can vouch for me. I went straight to her house. Does Max think I did that?"

"I don't know, Zena. You will have to talk to Max."

"Okay, Sadie. I will. I am truly sorry again about the other day," Zena humbly stated.

"No problem. It is now water under the bridge Zena." Zena seemed to be not telling me the whole story about her and Max. Why do I keep getting this feeling there was more to this story?

"I appreciate that, Sadie." Zena leaned over and whispered, "I don't play nice sometimes."

"I can tell," I whispered back.

Colby was ready to go by the time we got back to the room.

"All okay girls?" Colby cracked, twirling and snapping his fingers.

We looked at each other simultaneously saying, "We're good."

Finally, I took Queen Colby home. Colby entered the apartment slowly. He seemed a little sluggish. Colby laid on the couch rubbing his head. The cheerfulness was starting to calm, and the pain pills were starting to work.

"How is your head, Colby?" I asked as I handed him a full plate of spaghetti with garlic bread on the side.

"It is fine, Sadie. Only a slight pain where the stitches are but the headache is pretty much gone. This looks delicious, Sadie." Colby smiled.

I poured Colby a glass of water and me a glass of wine. It was not a good idea for Colby to mix wine with pain medication. Colby made it very clear a glass of wine would taste wonderful with that plate of good food. I stood my ground and told him no. He put on his cute pout like Max.

It was close to 8:30 p.m. and Max wasn't home yet.

Colby finished up his last few bites and patted his belly. "Oh my God, Sadie! That is a sin, almost better than sex, girl. Girl! You can cook. Who taught you to cook like that?"

"Mostly my mama, but I learned some on my own," I replied as I gathered the dirty dishes up.

Max's plate was still sitting on the counter waiting for her. I was also waiting on her. I filled the sink up with soapy water and placed the dirty dishes in to soak.

"Baby girl, leave them. I can get them later," Colby screamed from the living room.

"I got them. You need to relax. Ouch, damn it!" I said pulling my hand out of the water fast.

"You okay?" Colby popped up off the couch looking over at me.

"Yeah, I just cut myself on a knife in the water like a stupid idiot. It is not bad. I just need a Band-Aid," I yelled back as I wrapped it in a paper towel."

"Max probably has some in her room. Look in the top drawer of her dresser," Colby yelled out.

Entering Max's room, I came to a sudden stop. I looked over at the bed and flashes of Max on top of me filled my thoughts. I could remember her intense moans. It felt like Max really wanted me. I could not believe that somebody actually wanted me. I picked up Max's pillow and wrapped my arms around it. I inhaled deeply taking in Max's scent.

"Can you find them, Sadie?" Colby was yelling, bringing me back to reality as I looked at the paper towel wrapped around my finger.

"Yes, Colby! I will be right there," I yelled back.

I pulled the top dresser drawer open. I saw the Band-Aids in the back of the drawer. There was something else that caught my eyes, a box of needles lying in the drawer.

Now, my mind was wondering what was going on. Why did Max need needles? I picked the box up looking at it and didn't see a prescription. Was Max doing drugs? I placed the box of needles back into the drawer and stared at them for a few minutes. Then I got it together and grabbed a Band-Aid, slowly closing the drawer watching the needles disappear.

"Found it!" I said as I entered the living room again. "Do you need anything, Colby?"

"Yes. I need to chat with you. Those nurses last night were boring," Colby smiled as he patted the couch for me to sit down."

Sitting down, I crossed my legs. "Okay Colby, what would you like to talk about?"

"Life!" he said.

Now, my inner thoughts were starting to panic for a moment. Then I just calmed down, thinking to myself I could handle this. Colby loved to talk, so I just needed to keep him talking about other stuff and not me.

"So, Colby, how did you and Max meet?"

Colby got excited about the question and sat up crossing his legs.

"Well, actually, we have been friends since we were little. Max was ten years old when we met, and I was seven. We were stuck together like glue. Where you saw Colby, you also saw Maxine and vice versa. Max always defended me from bullies in school. She was a scrappy little kid, scared of nothing and I feared everything. We knew each other was gay before we knew ourselves. It killed us when we were separated. We met in a small town just like Pulse in the state of Georgia. But then our families moved in different directions. My parents moved to Virginia, and Maxine's aunt and uncle moved to Texas. Maxine lived with them because her parents had been killed in an automobile accident."

Colby paused to take a sip of water.

"We always kept in touch and saw each other during the summer. Max would stay with my family in Virginia in a town about 100 miles from here. We have always been able to tell each other everything except there has been one thing Max doesn't talk to me about. One summer when we got together something was not right. Max wasn't the same. To this day she says it was my imagination, but I am not stupid. I know my Maxine, and there was something she has not and will not tell me."

"How did you and Max end up here in Pulse?" I asked to keep Colby talking.

Colby shifted a little on the couch.

His tone became a little softer. "When I was in my earlier twenties I was in love with the sweetest man. Our relationship was so perfect. It was like a beautiful fairytale. He was tall, with the darkest black hair, nice body, and deep blue eyes like the ocean. He truly loved me, and I loved him."

Colby reached over to the coffee table and grabbed his wallet. Reaching inside the wallet, he pulled out a picture. A picture of him and a man in each other's arms. Snow was falling in the background.

"This is Albert, my one true love of a lifetime." I was in love with him, and he loved me.

Colby paused running his finger over the picture.

I placed my hand on his knee.

"Albert died from complications of AIDS. He became HIV positive from a previous relationship. Please don't be scared for me because Albert was one of the cleanest, neatest men I have ever met. Even before I knew he was HIV positive, he would always clean up behind himself and very adamant about us having safe sex. I thought that was weird, but I never questioned it because our relationship was different. We enjoyed life to the fullest when we were together. There was nothing we didn't talk about, and when we were together, it seemed like no one else in the world existed. We could sit and talk and laugh for hours." Colby chuckled…. "We would get so sad and almost about to cry when we had to leave each other. Wherever you see Albert, you would see me. We always said, when we retire, we would get a convertible, put the top back and travel the world, just him and me. Our hearts really beat as one. I had started noticing a change in his health, but he always said, "I will be all right." When Albert finally got to the point where the disease was spreading quickly, he broke down and told me about AIDS. The doctors had prescribed a lot of experimental drugs with a lot of different side effects, but his immune system was just getting weaker. He was a handsome young-looking man when we met, and as the disease progressed it took over his body, and he began to age, spots on his face and uncontrollable bowels." *Tears started to run down Colby's eyes, and his voice was cracking, but he continued.* "I was still determined that I was going to be with him until the end. To make sure I could take care of him, I told Max. She immediately packed her things up and moved here to help me take care of him. Max never left my side the entire time. After Max arrived, Albert lasted about another eight months." *Colby placed his hand on my knee.* "Let me tell you this Sadie, even though society may say negative things about people with AIDS, they need to understand that you cannot get the disease by touching or being around someone. Everyone needs to be educated on the disease because it is just like cancer, it has no cure. People dealing with any disease just needs family and friends' support with unconditional love to help them through their journey." *Colby could barely talk because the tears were rolling down his face.*

"I am so sorry for your loss, Colby."

"No, no! There is no need to feel sorry for me. I am truly blessed to have had Albert in my life for the time I was given. He made me who I am. Most of all, I was loved unconditionally, and I was in love."

Colby wiped the tears away. "Now, I'm truly blessed to have Max. That is why I would never let anything happen to her. None of her friends would either. I can tell you; Max likes you, Sadie. But Max cannot afford to have a repeat of her and Zena's relationship. You do know they were together for about three years?"

"Yes, Max told me they were a couple, and it was complicated, so it didn't last," I replied.

With a hesitant voice, Colby said, "Is that all she told you?"

"Yes. Is there more because Zena and Lacey acted surprised when I said that to them, or they acted like there was more to the story."

Colby became quiet and looked away from me.

"Colby, what is it."

Colby took a deep breath. "Zena tore Max's heart into pieces. Max doesn't love just anyone. She has had her fill of women, but she doesn't just commit to a person at random. Zena was the only girl I knew of that she had ever loved until now. I am starting to see something there between you two."

I started to blush. "Maybe there is, but it is too early yet. What did Zena do?"

"Zena cheated on her with some scant in the next city. Max was destroyed, and she lost it."

"What do you mean Max lost it?"

There was a pause of silence before Colby answered.

"Max tried to kill herself, Sadie. It took Lacey, Tori and myself to get Max back healthy. She was in a very bad way. She wasn't talking to us, and we had no idea she was being eaten up the way she was. To my surprise, I wasn't aware of how gone Max really was. I blamed myself every day because I didn't see it coming. I just didn't know. It hurt me that I, Max's best friend, didn't know it was so bad that she would swallow a bottle of sleeping pills. We didn't know Max thought her only way out was to die. What type of friends are we? Max almost died that day, and so did I. There has been no one until you came along. So, Max needs to be happy, she deserves to be happy, and I can see you are doing that. We just can't lose her again."

I put my hand over my mouth and tried to hold back the tears.

I finally had to ask, "Colby, is it because of Zena that Max is using drugs?"

Looking surprised at the question. Colby said, "Max doesn't do drugs. What would make you think that?"

I admitted to seeing the needles in her room.

Colby laughed a little.

"Don't laugh at this. I will be here for her if she needs help."

"My dear Sadie! Max doesn't do drugs. She is a type one diabetic. She is on insulin."

Oh my God. I am such a fool.

I put my hands over my face again.

I don't know why I assumed it was a drug addiction. My own mama was a diabetic. I should have figured it out.

"It is okay, Sadie. You couldn't have known. All that I'm asking is, please be good to Max. It seems like she is falling hard for you," Colby said as he wrapped me in a big hug.

Finally, Max opened the door. Catching Colby and me in an embrace, Max stared for a moment.

"Should I be worried?"

Colby winked at me as he pulled away. "I don't think so, Max!"

Max has on a white t-shirt and blue overalls with one of the clips undone and that side of the overalls dropped down. She and those damn undone buttons make me go crazy for her and overalls make her look so sexy. I jumped off the couch and walked over to her. Max just scooped me up in her arms.

"You feel so good," Max whispered in my ear.

"Come and eat. I made spaghetti for everyone tonight." I kissed Max's cheek softly.

"Let me go in my room for a second, and I will be right back."

"Well, I am going to bed. Good night all," Colby said as he headed out the room.

"Love you, my queen! Glad you are home," Max yelled back.

A few minutes went by, and Max did not come back. I decided to go check in on her. Max was sitting on the end of the bed with the needle and insulin beside her. I walked in quietly and fell to Max's knees in front of her.

"Hey, you okay?" I asked as I looked into her eyes.

"Sorry, I am coming," Max said.

I reached over and grabbed the needle.

"Is this the proper dose, Max?"

Max shook her head yes.

"Where do you want it given, in your stomach or thigh?"

"Stomach," Max spoke softly.

I undid the clip on Max overalls and pulled them down. Max laid back gently on the bed. I gently lifted Max's shirt to expose her belly. Speaking softly, I told Max I knew how to do this. I help my mama with her insulin shots. I told Max just relax, as I kissed her lips softly. Max closed her eyes. A small moan released from her.

Placing the needle in the insulin bottle, I drew the liquid into the needle. I tapped the needle a few times and ripped open the alcohol wipe with my teeth. Running the swab over Max's stomach, I leaned over blowing on the area gently to dry the skin. I inserted the needle into the flesh, injecting the insulin slowly then pulling the needle out gently.

"Now you need to eat. Come on."

Max ate the entire plate within minutes, stopping only a few times to tell me how good the dinner was. I collected the dirty dish then placed it in the sink. I walked over and rubbed Max's shoulders.

"Max, you are exhausted. Let's get bathed and get you to bed."

I undressed Max in the bathroom. Then I got undressed. I started the water letting it get steamy hot. Stepping into the shower, the water ran over our bodies. Max pulled me closer kissing me softly. Her mouth trailed down to my nipples kissing them softly. I lifted Max's face with my fingers pulling her mouth away from my nipples. It took all I had to pull her mouth away from me. Even though it was feeling so damn good, I told Max not tonight baby. "Let's just bathe and get in bed because I know you are exhausted."

Max whispered, "Stay with me."

"I will."

Getting out of the shower, I dried Max's sexy body off, thinking to myself, Boy, I want to fuck her, but I knew she needed to get some rest.

Once we got out of the shower, we got in bed. I let Max lay on my chest. I wrapped my arms around her holding her close. In my mind, I kept replaying Colby's words. She tried to kill herself. I just laid in the dark feeling Max's body get heavy as hell as she fell asleep.

9

"Damn it! I can't believe this. Sadie fucking knows? Jesus! Sadie fucking knows."

—Max

It was finally Thursday, and that meant Max was on her last day of twelve-hour shifts. Just thinking got me excited that Friday was almost here, and I could spend time with Max at the softball game and after party. I was watching the clock every few minutes. It was only noon, and I had four more hours of work. Every so often, Mr. Mahoney gave me a piece of work to do. Staring out the window, I started to daydream about the weekend coming. The streets were empty except for an old station wagon and a blue van. The phone rang making me jump and spill water everywhere. The water was spreading across the desk and into a pile of paperwork Mr. Mahoney just gave me.

"Damn it!" I started fussing as I tried to pick up the telephone and papers at the same time....

"Law Office of Mo Mahoney," I answered.

The woman's voice on the phone said, "Hey bubbles! How have you been?"

I did not know who this lady was talking about. So, I told her, "I am sorry, but you have the wrong number. This is a law office."

"Are you sure, you are not bubbles? You sound just like bubbles."

"No, I am not bubbles." The frustration was apparent in my voice. This lady was frustrating me to the point I spilled water all over the papers on my desk.

Once again, the lady said, "Kate Ward, aka bubbles, stop playing with me."

"Ma'am my name is Sadie Jones, not Kate Ward or bubbles."

Then the line went dead. Looking at the telephone receiver, I mumbled out, "Bitch."

"Everything okay, Sadie?" Mr. Mahoney asked as he appeared in the doorway.

"Yes sir, a lady with the wrong number. I spilled my water, but the paperwork survived."

Mr. Mahoney turned and walked back into his office

mumbling. "Just relax, Sadie! I swear there is something different about you lately." His door closed shut.

The blue van sat on the street with the driver's window cracked…. Smoke blew out floating into the air every so often. The blue van woman was on the telephone, tapping her long nails on the window waiting for the boss to answer.

A man's voice came on, "Yeah, go ahead."

The blue van woman started to talk. "Seems she is working at a law office in town as the secretary. She is using the name Sadie Jones. I did as you asked and gave her a scare the other day. What do you want me to do next, boss?"

Click, click, click could be heard through the phone from the angry man on the other end.

"The name of the woman she is lying with is what I need. I will be arriving soon, and I want to make sure she suffers too."

The woman heard the phone slam down in her ear. Throwing the cigarette out the window, the van moved slowly down the street.

The factory lunch bell sounded. Max and Tori were meeting at their spot. They tried to eat together often, always making fun of what the other one brought for lunch. Tori got there first, and Max came walking over.

"Hey Tori, glad today is Thursday."

"Me too, bud. Want some sardines?" Tori asked holding up the little fish.

"Hell no! How do you eat those things? How does Lacey let you kiss her?" Max giggled.

Tori leaned over and made a kissy face to Max.

"Nasty!" Max pushed Tori's face away.

"So, how is it going with Sadie, Max?" Tori asked.

"It is going so good, Tori. I really like her. The sex is hot! We haven't seen each other since Monday, but we text throughout the day and night. She found out I am type one diabetic. I am sure Colby ran his mouth as usual. She is cool about it. She even gave me my shot the other day." Max just smiled like a kid in love.

"Why wouldn't she be, Max?" Tori asked.

"You know how Zena freaked out over the shots and illness," Max replied.

"Well…Zena is an idiot about it. Diabetes is just a disease. It's not like she could catch it." Tori snapped back.

"Tori, do you think Colby told Sadie about me trying to end my life?" Max asked.

"So, what if he did, Max? Colby only said something because he cares."

"You said he only said it? Tori, you knew he did? Damn it! I can't believe this. Sadie fucking knows? Jesus! Sadie fucking knows."

Max started to have a problem breathing. Her body started to rock back and forth. Tori has seen this many of times. Max was going into a panic attack. Tori wrapped her arms around her shoulder.

"Max, look at me. Look at me, Max. Sadie finding out didn't make her run. She has texted you all week. Right? Sadie is still coming to the game and party tomorrow with you. Right? It didn't scare her off. Now, take a deep breath for me, Max, and just calm down."

Max breathed in hard and then blew it out slowly. "I can't do this Tori," Max said as she started to rock harder.

"Max! Do you like this girl? I think Sadie likes you. I am sure she has some skeletons in her closet that you will be finding out about."

Max started thinking. Her thoughts went back to the night Sadie spaced out on her, and she had forgotten to ask her about it.

That night got crazy with Colby in the hospital, and then Zena acting out. It just slipped her mind to ask Sadie. Max's breathing became normal. "I can do this."

"Yes! Max, you can do this," Tori responded.

"Okay, okay Tori," Max said shaking her head yes. "I am going to invite Sadie to the cabin this weekend and try to stay to Monday since I am already off. Just need for Sadie to call in sick on Monday. I plan on getting her to open up to me, and I am going to try to be open too."

"That will be great for you and her, Max. I am sure it will be a great and exciting time away. If you need anything from me, please let me know," Tori said.

"No, I am good and thanks, Tori, for always being here for me."

"Also, don't be mad at Colby. He only did what we all wanted to do. We just wanted Sadie to know what you had been through. We are just trying to find out if she is playing you. Max, I need to ask a favor of you," Tori's toned changed, and she wanted to change the subject.

"You can ask me anything, Tori. Always!"

Tori paused before she reached into her pocket. Pulling out a jewelry box, she opened it revealing a large diamond. "I am asking Lacey to marry me, and I need you to be my best person?"

"*Hell yeah*! I will be glad to stand beside you. That's awesome, Tori. I am happy for you," Max sounded out in excitement.

"She has to say yes first."

"After ten years of being together why wouldn't she?"

"Well…you know how our fights can get very heated," Tori answered.

"Lacey really loves you, Tori. Your fights didn't make her run." Max smiled. "Your words!"

Tori placed the little box back in her pocket. "Max, you are right. That is true."

"Hey Max, we are ahead of the production so do you want to get off around two?"

"Yes, Tori. Thanks!"

"Love you, girl."

"Love ya back, girl, but keep them damn sardines away from me."

I was sitting at my desk watching a clock with hands that looked like they were not moving. I lowered my head burying my face in my hands. Whispering aloud to myself in a low voice, "I am dying here. I'm ready to go."

Then I heard a voice, "Can I get a kiss before you die?"

To my surprise, Max was standing in front of my desk. All I could do was smile. Damn, she has on those overalls and white shirt again that she looks SOOO good in.

In those clothes, Max just drove me out of my mind.

So, now I'm curious. "What are you doing here, Max?" Not trying to be so obvious, I glanced around to make sure I did not see Mr. Mahoney.

Luckily, that day, Mr. Mahoney had been in and out of the office. Thinking about the time, and since I did not see him, this was the normal time he went to the restroom doing his daily stinky business. It was every day at 2:30 pm. You could set your clock by him. So, after looking around, I rushed around the desk.

"Max, you are off work already?"

Max looked me up and down. "You know you are driving me crazy in this skirt." Max leaned into me causing me to sit on the desk. She looked down, tracing the inside of my thigh, her fingers grazing upward slipping under my skirt.

"Max, don't!" I grabbed Max's hands to try to stop them from moving any farther. Don't get me wrong. The thought of fucking Max on the desk was going through my mind, but I didn't want Mr.

Mahoney to walk in on us.

"I will stop if you go to dinner with me."

"Fine, I will go to dinner with you. But you need to get out of here before I get in trouble."

"I will pick you up. Oh, and Sadie, wear this skirt minus these." Max slipped her hand under my skirt and rolled her finger under the lace panties I had on. Max slipped my panties down, then she bent over and lifted my foot helping me step out of them.

I can't believe Max put my panties in her pocket, smiled and said see you at six.

I just sat at my desk in a daze watching Max and my panties walk out the door, thinking how bad I wanted to go with her because my vagina was ready.

Finally, it was time for me to get off work. I rushed home to take a shower. Boy, did I need one after Max left me wet as hell today. Slipping the same skirt back on with a new top, I was ready. I went outside to wait patiently for Max to come around the corner. A few minutes later, Max pulled in front of Mrs. Preakness' house right at 6:00 pm. I jumped in the car closing the door behind me. I just looked over at Max and smiled.

"What Sadie?" Max smiled back at me.

"One of us is overdressed. I must say, Max, those sweatpants and t-shirt sure look sexy on you."

"Yeah, and that skirt really looks sexier on you," Max said while smiling.

Max drove the car curving it down the dark road. We were headed out of town toward the city. A car passed every so often, reminding us that we were not alone in the world. Max held my wrist the entire drive, rubbing her thumb softly over my skin. The windows were down and the night air was flowing in the car. I was so relaxed it felt like my body was melting into the seat. We breathed in the night air and exhaled slowly. Max tighten her grip and pulled my hand up and kissed it softly.

Max turned the car down a dirt road. I started to look around curiously.

"Where are we going?" I asked.

"We are here," Max replied as the car pulled into an open area.

Pulling up to the wooden fence, Max turned off the car. The city lights lit the whole sky in front of us. There were a few cars parked around that were sharing the same beautiful night. Everyone was spread out just enough not to invade each other's space. Only figures and shadows could be seen in the cars moving and intertwining together.

Max covered the hood with a thick blanket. She helped me up on the hood. She laid out the picnic spread comprised of fruits, cracker, cheese and deli meat. Lying on our sides facing each other, we fed each other, as we laughed while flirting with each other.

"It is so beautiful up here," I said slowly as I slipped a grape in Max's mouth.

"It is but can be very dangerous. Two people were making out, and they hit the gear shift causing the car to roll off the ledge. That's why I parked here. If the car starts to roll it will contact the little wooden fence in front of us, but it will not stop the car if it has too much speed." Max slipped another grape into my mouth. Then I jumped off the hood looking over the ledge down into the black hole.

Max jumped off the hood and pulled me back into her arms. She leaned on the car with me leaning back on her. She pulled the back of my hair up covering the back of my neck with little butterfly kisses. Whispering over my neck, Max said, "I missed you."

I just closed my eyes and enjoyed every moment of the attention Max was giving me. I could tell Max's body was full of excitement.

Max spun me around toward her, her lips softly caressing mine, sucking gently over them. Pulling away, Max whispered, "You are so addicting, Sadie. Go away with me this weekend and Monday to a cabin in the mountains."

Max paused for a bit. "I want to open up to you. I want to tell you about…" Max took a breath. "This is harder than I thought."

I wrapped our fingers together holding both of our hands between us. "I would love to go away with you, Max. I will have to figure out Monday. So, for now, let's just enjoy this beautiful night together."

I moved Max's hand down to her thighs, pressing her palm into her leg. Max kissed me, letting our lips move over each other making them moist. Our lips got lost in each other.

The car suddenly jerked forward. The sound of glass shattering echoed in the night. Max and I were thrown off the car. Max fell to the ground, but I flew into the wooden fence hitting a post hard with my back. I just laid there for a moment with the wind knocked out of me. Max jumped up and ran over to me kneeling on the ground beside me.

"Jesus, Sadie! Are you okay?" Max asked as she helped me sit up.

At that point, I could only shake my head yes as I tried to catch my breath. I was finally able to speak. "I am okay. What happened, Max?"

"Stay here," Max said.

Max stood up and noticed a woman looking at the back of the car. As Max started to walk toward the woman, the woman started to speak. "I am so sorry. I had my van in reverse instead of drive, and it got away from me. I was turning around because I took the wrong road. I am sure my insurance will take care of everything."

Max looked at the damage.

The woman's blue van took most of the hit from the impact. The taillight on the woman's van is broken, but Max's car had a dented trunk. I was standing up by now. I could only see the figure of the person Max was talking to.

"Let's just exchange names and insurance," Max said.

"Is your friend okay?" the woman asked.

Max looked back toward me. "She is fine."

The woman and Max exchanged insurance information.

"Once again, I am so sorry Ms. Shields," the lady said as she looked over the information. "I am sure it will get fixed."

"I am sure," Max replied.

The woman climbed into the blue van and Max watched the broken taillight drive away in the dark. People stopped what they were doing to look but soon resumed their activities. I walked up behind Max wrapping my arms around her and looking over at the damage.

"Everything okay, Max?" I asked.

"Yes," Max replied as she turned to me.

"Did you know the lady, Max? Her voice sounded familiar."

"No, I do not know her. Are you sure you are okay, Sadie? That was a hard hit you took," Max asked in a concerned voice.

"I am fine. It just knocked the wind out of me."

Max pulled me into a hug. "Let's clean the food up."

We wrapped all the picnic stuff up placing it in the dented trunk. Max kissed me on the cheek as she slammed the trunk closed. Grabbing my wrist, Max guided me to the front door of the car and opened it for me. I closed the door. Opening the back door, I slipped inside. Max smiled and slipped in behind me.

I looked over at Max and asked her, "What do you want?" Max laid her hand on my thigh, with her fingers did circles. Max reached into her pocket pulling my panties out. "Are these still missing?"

"Is that what you want to know, Max?"

"Yes, Sadie, that's what I want!"

I hiked my skirt up revealing my vagina.

Max took my hand and placed it on my vagina. "Touch yourself, Sadie!" Max whispered as she watched.

I slipped my finger into my vagina. I closed my eyes and laid my head back. Max sat there just watching, getting a glance at my vagina as I spread my vagina wide open with every roll of my finger. Max started to shift a little as she felt her vagina awaken. Raising my shirt up over my breasts, she let my breasts fall free.

"Make your nipples hard Sadie."

Max watched as I cupped my breast. I pulled at my nipple, biting my lower lip as it became hard. I opened my eyes; Max was engrossed in watching me. She was touching her own breast.

Max groaned. "Oh…Sadie, moan for me."

My fingers rolled harder around my clit. I arched a little into my hand. "Ah…baby"

Max leaned over to my ear, whispering, "You have me SOOO wet. Let me see you pull your nipples harder."

I pulled my nipples while moaning Max's name. Max moaned out with me. I was so into how my finger was making me feel; I didn't even notice Max had slipped her sweats and panties off.

Max leaned back over whispering again in my ear, "Slip your finger inside yourself again."

Max watched as I slowly dipped my finger deep inside my vagina. My legs closed as I lifted my hips into my hands. Max spread my legs back apart. "I want to see you." My breathing was getting heavier, and my moans were getting closer together.

Max leaned over, "What do you want, Sadie?" she whispered.

I almost exploded when I heard her words. "YOU," I moaned out.

Max grabbed my wrist and slowly pulled my fingers from deep inside my vagina. "Ah…" I groaned.

"Don't cum yet, Sadie," Max whispered.

Max pulled me over onto her lap laying my wet vagina on hers. "Pull my shirt up," Max gasped. I exposed Max's breasts, covering them both with my palms. I started to rub her breasts softly. Max started to grind slowly, both of our moans started to fill the car.

Max placed her thumb between our vaginas, pressing hard on our clits. Ah, shit, this was feeling so good. I raised up and starting to grind. The motion of moving fast back and forth was igniting our vaginas even more.

She stopped the grinding. She pushed me back, so I was leaning on the back of the front seat. I was breathing hard. I was so close.

"Max, please don't stop."

Max spread my legs apart tracing her fingers over me. I was so wet. Max was breathing hard. "Watch me, Sadie."

Max slipped her hand down between her own legs, her head laying back as her finger slipped in. Fuck I am on fire. "OH God," Max groaned loudly. "Touch yourself again, Sadie."

My finger slipped back inside of me, my eyes on Max as she masturbated. "Max."

Max was arching hard. "OH, Sadie, cum with me."

With my back arched I released. Hearing Max's words sent me over the edge. I moaned out, "Yes!"

I felt Max release at the same time. "Oh. Sadie!"

Our bodies were twisting with more than one explosion erupting. I finally collapsed on top of Max. We both were breathing hard and heavy unable to talk. Max just wrapped her arms around me, holding me tight. We were not able to do anything but sit there and gather ourselves.

❧

The blue van woman pulled over to make a phone call to her boss. Her boss had been waiting for her call.

"Go ahead," the man demanded.

"The girl's name is Maxine Shields, and she lives at 207 Grayson Road."

"Good. Now the games will begin," he said before the line went silent.

10

"You play hard in the game, and we can play harder later."
—Sadie

Max pulled up into the driveway of the house. Turning off the engine, she turned to me and ran her fingers over my cheek.

"Are you sure I can't talk you into going back to my place tonight, Sadie?" Max asked.

"Not tonight, Max. I must work tomorrow, and you need to sleep in. I can tell you are tired; you need some rest. Plus, I need to get a few things together for the weekend. I promise I will go back to your place tomorrow after the party."

"I will sleep better with you in my bed," Max whispered as she played with my hair.

"I doubt sleeping will be on your mind." I gave Max a smirk.

Max smiled. "Probably not. I am looking forward to this weekend, spending the nights with you, then waking up with you in the morning. If it wasn't the last party of the softball season, I would skip it and leave with you as soon as you get off work."

"I am looking forward to this weekend also. Must admit I am a little nervous about the party."

"Why, Sadie? All my girls including Colby really like you," Max replied.

"I guess," slipped out of my lips.

"Sadie?"

"I am sorry, Max. It will be fun. I haven't been to a party in ages."

Max looked at the front door of the house. "Do you know your boss bangs the lady that lives here with you? I think her name was Felicia. The lady wears a lot of makeup and perfume."

"My boss is doing the perfume lady. Really? Mr. Mahoney? Ewe that's nasty. Geesh, now I have a visual."

We just busted out laughing. At the same time, we both said, "Nasty." Laughter broke out again.

"I have fun with you, Sadie."

Max leaned over, her lips finding my soft, moist lips, small pecks erupting into soft sucks erupting into tongues slipping in and out. I unbuckled myself climbing over on top of Max. I reached over and unbuckled Max, our lips never separating as the kiss became deeper and deeper. Moans were escaping our mouths again as we both grasped at each other's breasts.

"Shit, Sadie, I just can't get enough of you," Max moaned over my lips.

Suddenly, the driver's door flew open. I pulled away from Max's lips stepping out of the car.

"Where are you going?" Max asked as she tried to pull me back.

I leaned into the car letting our lips connecting and then slipping apart. "I am going to pack, and you are going to go home and get some rest. See you tomorrow and thanks for tonight."

"You know that is just cruel and wrong Sadie." Max smiled. "Night, sweetie!"

"Night, Max!" I replied while smiling.

The next day, Max slept in until 10:00 am. When she woke, she was excited about the weekend and Monday plans. Tori was picking her up at noon to go shopping for the party. Lacey made sure Tori had a big long list and strict instructions on what to get. By 11:45am, Max was ready and sitting outside the apartment complex when Tori's truck rolled into the parking lot.

"Hey, Tori," Max said as she jumped into the truck.

Tori was looking at Max like something was wrong. Her face was sad.

"Oh, Tori, what happened?" Max asked.

"Well, I asked Lacey to marry me?" Tori answered looking away.

"Don't tell me she said no, Tori."

Tori turned to Max and took a deep breath, "Hell no," she said, "YES!"

"You bitch!" Max pushed Tori on the shoulder. "I am thrilled for you. You might as well marry her. She has your ass whipped anyhow," Max said jokingly.

"True that, Max." Tori laughed.

Tori and Max arrived at the grocery store. They walked around picking up odds and ends for the party. They were on the chip aisle. "Grab some plain chips, Max. Make sure it is Ms. Potato Chip brand. That is the only one Lacey likes." Max made a whipping gesture with her hands followed by the noise. Tori smiled and lifted her middle finger up to her.

"We also need to get some dip. I think it is in the next aisle," Tori said as she threw a bag of corn chips in the basket.

Max wheeled the basket around the corner and slammed into another basket. All the groceries shifted in the cart, the sound of glass clanging into each other filled the air.

"I am sorry," Max said as she looked up. "Hey, you are the lady from last night," Max said.

"I see we have had another accident, Ms. Shields." The lady pointed to Max's cart. A jar of pickles was leaking, and the juices were slowly dripping to the floor.

"Damn," Tori said as she reached into the cart to get the broken jar. "I will have to go get some help to clean up this mess and then get some more pickles." Tori took off down the aisle.

"I reported the accident as soon as I got home last night. I am sure my insurance company will be calling you soon about that dented trunk. How is Sadie?" the woman asked.

"She is fine but how did you know her name?" Max asked looking with a strange expression on her face.

"You must have told me last night," the woman stated. "Have a nice day, Maxine." The woman walked quickly away leaving Max there in the middle of the aisle. Tori walked up and watched the lady walking away.

"What's up with Cruella de Vil wannabe?" Tori asked.

"That lady hit my car last night. Sadie and I were at Lover's Peak last night, and she backed into my car."

"Lover's Peak, huh?" Tori nudged Max.

"Yeah, yeah." Max smiled.

"Max? You good?" Tori laid her hand on Max's shoulder.

"I am better than good, Tori."

"Great! Now, can we please get this shit on this list that Lacey gave me done and get the hell out of here?" Tori giggled.

The sound of a whip could be heard again from Max.

At the office, I had my back to the door while I was filing some papers. I heard the door open. So, I shouted out from the corner, "I will be right with you." Closing the file cabinets, I turned around. "Hi, Lacey. What are you doing here?" I asked.

Lacey smiled, "I am here for you. My car is in the alley. I will be waiting for you. Go tell your boss you are not feeling well and you need to go home."

"What?" I said with a puzzled look on my face.

"I already know you and Max are going away through Monday and you are going to call in sick. So be sick now and meet me in the alley, Sadie."

The sound of Mr. Mahoney's door opening suddenly made me jump.

"Hurry," Lacey said as she exited out the door.

Mr. Mahoney entered the office reading some papers.

"Mr. Mahoney, I'm not feeling well, so I think I will be taking off a half day," I stumbled out.

"That's fine. Feel better, Sadie." He never looked up from his papers as he walked back into his office.

Lacey was sitting in her car when I walked up. "Come on, get in!" she ordered.

I leaned in the window. "What is going on Lacey?"

"Just get in, Sadie."

I finally jumped in the car closing the door behind me. "So, now will you tell me where we are going?"

Lacey put on a pair of big sunglasses and then she smiled. "We are getting you a makeover."

I just looked over at her with a surprised look. Lacey threw her car into drive then peeled out. Lacey pulled in front of the beauty salon. I looked up and turned to Lacey.

"No. Not here," I said in a panic voice. I looked back at the store then back at Lacey. "NO!"

"Sadie, she offered. This was all her idea. She would never do anything to hurt your hair. I promise, and I will be here the whole time. Don't insult her by not accepting."

I just sat there for a minute. "Jesus," I mumbled as Lacey swung the car door open.

"Gonna be fun." Lacey clapped her hands together.

Zena waved us over to a chair as soon as we walked in the door. Her shop was nicely decorated with a calming atmosphere. There were two other hairdressers in the shop. They waved to Lacey as we headed to the chair.

"Hello, Lacey" Zena hugged her.

"Hey Sadie," she flipped my hair around looking at it. "Ready for something new, Sadie?" Zena asked.

"Um…not to new," I said with a little unsureness in my voice.

"Don't worry, Sadie; I will keep it subtle." Zena patted the chair.

Zena washed my hair and then put conditioner on it. She talked me into letting her put light highlights of blonde through my hair. I was stressing the entire time the dye was in my hair. I also agreed to let her cut at least two inches off the length then layer it. Lacey and Zena did most of the talking. The subjects bounced from the party to who Zena had screwed lately. I didn't bring up Max or the upcoming weekend, and I was really hoping Lacey kept her lips shut about it. Zena spun the chair around so I could look in the mirror.

"Now, that is a sexy cut," Zena said with pride.

"Oh my God, Zena. I don't even look like myself." I was admiring my new haircut.

"You are hot, Sadie. If I didn't have Tori, I would fuck you."

"Me too," Zena whispered in my ear.

Geesh! What was it with these girls. They both were beautiful women, but nothing compared to my Max. That's right, my Max. "Okay. Thanks so much, Zena." I ripped the smock off and jumped up. "How much do I owe you, Zena?"

"It is on the house. It is my peace offering."

"Thanks, Zena," I responded.

Lacey pulled me toward the door. Lacey turned around and winked at Zena. Zena half-waved then looked at herself in the mirror as she leaned on the chair. Zena slowly dropped her head.

I placed my suitcase in the car before I went to work. Max had told me I could change for the party at Tori and Lacey's house once the game was over. It was 3:30 and I decided to head over to Max's apartment. I wanted to leave the car at Max's apartment complex rather than in front of Mrs. Preakness' house. That would cut down on the time I will have to hear Mrs. Preakness bitch about the car being parked in front of her house.

So, I knocked on the door. Colby peaked around the open door.

"Girl! Look at your sexy ass. Now, that is hot. I know that work anywhere. That has Z written all over it. Has Max seen it?" Colby said as he showed his excitement.

I blushed. "No, not yet. You think she will like it, Colby?"

"Girl, she will love it."

Max walked out of the bedroom into the living room. Her head was down as she was trying to fix her softball shirt button in the right slot. I walked over and grabbed the button from her.

"Let me get this for you," I said softly. I slipped the button through the slit. "There you go."

Max looked up, her mouth curving into this huge smile. "I have never seen anyone as beautiful as you." She stepped into me and placed both her hands on the sides of my face. She drew me into a big kiss. It was soft and passionate. I just melted in Max's arms. Time seemed to go on forever when we were together.

"Hello?" Colby said as he cleared his throat.

Max pulled away from me slowly with her eyes still closed. Opening them, she stared at me for a moment. "I just love the new look. Who did it?"

"Zena did. Lacey pulled me out of work today for a makeover."

"She did a great job. I don't think I can play today. You will be too big of a distraction on the sidelines." Max smiled.

I leaned into Max's ear and whispered, "You play hard in the game, and we can play harder later."

Max swallowed, "What have I created?"

"Are y'all done? Can we get going, Ms. Thangs? We have some ass to kick on the field," Colby said as he picked up Max's bat bag.

At the field, I sat with Lacey on the bleachers. Colby was the batboy and hung out in the dugout. The game was a nailbiter. All night, the score went back and forth. Zena was pitching. Tori was the catcher. Max moved over to third base because the regular third base got hurt at work earlier in the week. Zena threw in the pitch, and the batter hit it hard past the pitcher's mound and into the open field. The batter took off at full speed, and it didn't look like she was going to stop. She rounded second then headed to third base at full speed. The ball was coming in from the outfield. The batter and the ball got to third base at the same time. Max caught the ball just as the batter slammed hard into her. Max's body flew in the air, hitting the dirt hard, the ball falling from her mitt. Her body went limp and still. Her eyes closed. I stood up in the bleachers, "Max," I screamed as I jumped down from the bleachers. Lacey followed me on my heels into the field. Colby was running out of the dugout. Tori and Zena reached Max and were calling her name. Max's body laid still. I pushed my way to Max. Kneeling beside her, I placed my hand on her forehead.

"Max, open your eyes. Max, Max, come on baby, look at me," I said as I started to cry.

Max suddenly arched her back. She engulfed the air. She reached up and pulled me into a kiss.

"She will be fine," Colby belted out.

"Jesus, you scared the fuck out of me!" I said in a fussing voice as I slapped her arm softly.

Tori helped Max sit up. "Ready to try to get up?" Tori asked.

Tori, Colby, Lacey and I helped Max get over to the dugout. Suddenly, Zena just lost it. "*Fuck This*! I need to kick some ass!" Marching over to the batter who just caused Max to be knocked out, she coldcocked her. The benches cleared and both teams were fighting in the middle of the field. Lacey and Tori ran back in to help Zena. The referee called the game and security finally came over to break all the women apart. There were scrapes, cuts and bruises on a lot of the women.

"You okay, Max?" I asked again.

"I am okay. My head never hit. The air was just knocked out of me, which made me pass out."

Tori walked back over holding a tissue on her nose. The blood was dripping down her lip. Lacey and Zena followed her. Zena was shaking her hand, and her knuckles started to swell.

"Let's get out of here," Tori said to the group.

11

"SWING LADIES."
—Colby

Max showered at Tori's house, and I changed into my black dress. It was one of my best dresses. It fit tightly and showed off all my curves. Max exited the shower in jeans and a white muscle shirt. The top button of her jeans was unbuttoned. Oh, yes, that was the look on Max that really turns me on.

"WOW, you look fantastic," Max said as she wrapped me up in her arms.

"Are you sure you are okay, Max?" I asked.

"I am fine, Sadie. I promise. Let's go party."

The whole group changed their clothes from softball attire to party wear. The party was in full force by the time we went downstairs. The music was booming, and Colby was running the turntables. Any sign of his head hurting was long gone. Colby was out in full force. He made me smile all the time. Tori and Lacey were doing the rounds saying hello to everyone. Zena picked up the model Lorraine for the party and was curled up in a lounge chair by the pool. They were doing shots off each other's breast.

Max grabbed a beer and handed it to me.

Tori and Lacey soon joined them. Lacey had a tray of shots.

"Want a shot, guys?" Lacey asked while forcing the glass in my hand. Max refused, but I didn't want to be rude. I tossed back the shot swallowing the hot liquid.

"That's a little warm." I started to cough.

"It is a fireball." Lacey just smiled.

"Your house is beautiful, Lacey. I love the pool area. It reminds me of the rainforest with all the live plants."

"We got a great deal. The previous owners needed to sell fast. Thank you," Lacey replied.

Tori looked at Max. "Are you okay, Max? That was a hard hit."

"It is all good, Tori."

Tori leaned over and whispered in Max's ear, "Time to let the family hear the news."

Tori jumped onto the diving board of the pool and pulled

Lacey up with her. Lacey handed the shot tray to me. Tori picked up the mic and motioned for Colby to kill the music.

"Can I have everyone's attention, please? Before everyone gets hammered, Lacey and I want to make an announcement. After ten years of love, fights, more love and then more fights…"

Laughter could be heard throughout the pool area.

"This crazy woman has said yes. Lacey has agreed to marry me and start a new chapter of our lives together."

Lacey held up her ring then leaned in and kissed Tori hard. The cheers filled the air as beer bottles clanged and everyone took a sip of their drink.

"Max has agreed to be my best person, and Zena has agreed to be Lacey's best person."

Again, everyone held their drinks up, and cheers erupted.

Max and Zena walked over to the newly engaged couple and hugged them. I watched them as I took another shot. Tilting the glass back, the second one went down smoother. The music fired back up filling the air with electricity. Max walked back over to me wrapping me in her arms. She kissed me softly.

"Want something to eat?" Max asked.

"Sure"

The kitchen and dining room were filled with tables that had everything you could ask for from chips, dips, wings, sandwiches and cheeses to veggies. Max and I filled our plates and sat to the side of the kitchen. We fed each other as we did the night before. Max tried to get me to eat some broccoli, but I closed my lips tight and shook my head no. I just smiled when I tried to feed Max some hummus, and she just tightened her lips.

I started to finish my second beer when I noticed Zena and Lorraine slipping up the stairs. I told Max I would be right back because I needed more crackers. Kissing Max softly, I got up with a little stumble.

"You okay, Sadie?" Max asked as she steadied me.

"I am okay. My heel caught the chair," I answered.

In the kitchen, I grabbed some crackers and noticed some Jell-O on a tray. I picked one up and tossed it back. Single serving how nice I thought. I grabbed two beers on my way back to join Max.

"You want a beer, baby?" I asked Max as I sat down.

"No thanks. I cannot drink a lot 'cause of my diabetes. It may hurt my kidneys. Plus, I am the DD." Max smiled wiping hummus off my mouth. I finished up the crackers and half of the third beer.

"I have to go to the bathroom. I will be right back," I said.

"I will meet you outside. I am going to go check on Tori and Colby." Max gave me a kiss.

I worked my way up the stairs to the bathroom. I closed the door behind me. Washing my face, I heard sounds coming from the adjacent bedroom. So, I cracked the door, and I could see an overlarge bed. I tried to focus my eyes because it was dark in the room. There was a woman thrusting herself over another woman. The moans were loud, and the woman on top had the other woman's arms pinned to the bed. The woman on the bottom had her legs wrapped around the waist of the woman on top. I could see the woman on top's ass in a steady rhythm grinding the woman on the bottom. The woman on top came up on her knees to get a better angle. The woman on the bottom was moaning almost in pain as the woman on top thrust hard into her. The covers slipped down farther, and I could see the belts around the woman's waist on top. Trying to see, I refocused my eyes when I see a penis. It was being driven into the woman on the bottom. The woman on the top started to thrust faster, and she moaned aloud when she exploded. The woman on the bottom followed her with her own explosion. I moved the door, and it creaked. The woman on top looked over, and I noticed it was Zena right before I shut the door and locked it. I just went to the bathroom as fast as I could manage before running downstairs.

I ran outside and right into Max's arms.

"You okay? You are flushed," Max said.

"Yes, it probably just the alcohol," I answered.

Max ushered me toward Colby. He was rocking the DJ job. The music was thumping hard.

"I need a drink, Max. Be right back," I yelled in Max's ear over the music. I went into the kitchen and grabbed a beer from the cooler. There was another woman in the kitchen with me.

The woman asked me if I am having fun. "Yes," I replied as I opened the beer drinking over half.

"Want a brownie?" the woman asked as she stepped closer to me.

I was now holding myself up by the counter. The woman slipped a piece of brownie in my mouth. I chewed the brownie slowly then swallowing.

"Want more?" the woman asked as she cornered me against the counter. The woman's fingers slipped another piece into my mouth. The woman's finger rolled over my lips. I closed my eyes then opened them back up as the room started to spin. The woman pushed me against the counter, placing her hands on my waist. The woman was leaning into me.

"Don't push me. Please back up."

"I think she said to back off, Megan. What are you doing, Sadie?" Zena asked sternly.

The brownie woman jumped off me.

"Getting a beer," I nervously replied. I am going to find Max. I mumbled out the words as I tried to walk away. Zena pushed me back on the counter. "Stay for a minute."

Zena turned to the brownie woman. "What is in these fucking brownies?" Zena picked one up and smelled it. The woman leaned over and whispered something in Zena's ear.

"You know this is Max's girl?" Zena was getting mad, and she stepped closer to the brownie woman. "Get the fuck out of here."

"Sadie, put the beer down. You have had enough."

"You can't boss me or Max," I barked back at Zena as I pushed past her.

Zena watched me walk out the door. I walked back over to Max and Colby. Colby was showing Max something about the turntable. Colby turned down the volume and picked up the microphone. Okay, ladies! It was time to SWING.

"What is that, Max?" I asked.

"We don't have to do it, Sadie. We line up and dance and when Colby yells SWING, we move one person over."

"That sounds like fun. Come on," I said as I pulled on Max.

Max followed and lined up across from me. The music started to thump hard. Max walked up to me and placed her hands on my hips. They started to sway slowly then faster as I wrapped my arms around her neck. Colby yelled out, "AND WE ARE SWINGING." Max slipped in front of Lacey and Tori grabbed me. Tori spun me around and almost had to hold me up.

"Sadie, you okay?" Tori asked.

Colby overpowered the noise, "SWING LADIES."

Tori didn't swing. She could tell something wasn't right with me. Max did swing and ended up with Zena. I held on to Tori's neck trying to balance myself. Looking and focusing on Max, I could see Zena.

The music was jamming, and Zena had her back to Max. They were grinding into each other to the music. Zena had her arms up and wrapped around Max's neck. Max had her chin buried into Zena's neck. Their bodies were moving as one.

I suddenly broke from Tori and ran off.

Tori went over to Max tapping her on the shoulder. "Go check on your girl!"

Max took off after me, leaving Zena with Tori. I hadn't gotten far. I did more stumbling than walking.

"Sadie, wait Sadie!" Max called out.

I stopped in my tracks. I am swaying back and forth as Max

walked up.

Max grabbed me and said, "What is going on?"

"I can't compete with Zena," I slurred out.

"There was no competition. It was just dancing Sadie. I didn't mean to upset you." Max tried to wrap her arms around me, but I just pulled away.

Max grabbed me back. "Don't pull away, Sadie!"

"Don't fucking grab me, Max! Don't crowd me!" I yelled at Max.

Max took a deep breath. She held out her hands for me to place my wrist in her hand. Max waited until I finally placed my wrist into her hand.

"Baby, how much have you had to drink?" Max asked as she stepped closer.

"Not enough."

"I think you have had quite a bit. You ready to go home with me?"

"No, I am going swimming."

"If you go swimming Sadie, I have to go swimming," Max said calmly.

"I saw the girls in the pool. We don't need a bathing suit. They are naked," I replied as I pushed past Max.

"Shit!" Max mumbled.

Taking steps sideways instead of straight to the pool. Max was following me. I pulled down my dress straps over my shoulders letting the dress fall to the ground. I kicked off my shoes and then the last to go was my panties before I hit the water. Tori and Zena stopped Max on the way to the pool. Max kept her eyes on me while she listened to them. "Megan gave Sadie some hard street hash in brownies earlier in the kitchen," Zena spilled.

"What?" Max yelled.

Max was still watching me in the pool. Zena said she tried to stop me, but it was too late because she had already eaten the brownie.

"What a bitch! I am going to kick Megan's ass!"

"You need to take care of Sadie," Tori told Max as she stopped her from going after Megan. Bracing Max's shoulders, Tori looked at Max. "Take care of your girl."

"Get me a blanket Tori and bring my car as close as you can," Max instructed as she took off her muscle shirt.

"Thank you, Zena," Max said as she passed Zena pulling her pants off.

Max dove into the pool and swam up to me. "Hey baby, what are you doing?"

"Taking a bath, you need a bath too?" Sadie's eyes were glassed over.

"I need you. Can we go home?" Max said.

"I need you too!" I laid a sloppy kiss on Max.

"Hey Max, did you know Zena has a penis?" I fell into Max in the pool. "Oops, I am a little clumsy.

"I don't doubt that baby. Look, Sadie. Tori has a towel for you to dry off." Max was trying to encourage me to the edge of the pool where Tori was standing with a blanket.

"Okay, I think I am clean now." I started to sway back and forth. She closed her eyes and collapsed into Max's arms.

Max scooped her up. Tori helped Max out of the pool. Wrapping the blanket around Sadie, Tori and Max carried her to the car. Zena, Lacey, and Colby grabbed our clothes from the lawn. Max grabbed her shirt and pants from Zena and dressed beside the car. Zena couldn't help but admire Max's body. She missed it. Colby climbed into the back seat with me.

"Thank you, guys. I am sorry about this." Max hugged everybody before she jumped in the car.

Max and Colby woke Sadie up just enough so she could

stumble into the apartment with their help. Max took her to the bedroom. She pulled the bedspread back and slipped her onto the bed. Max turned me on her side, placing a trashcan beside the bed, and a bottle of water with two aspirin.

Colby sat at the end of the bed. "Why did Sadie drink so much, Max?" Colby asked.

"I don't know, Colby," Max responded in a low voice.

Max pushed the hair out from the front of my face. I swiped at her hand and screamed out. "Don't touch me. Please, I won't do it again. STOP! NO!" she drifted back off to sleep. Max continued to rub her head.

"What the hell has this girl been through, Max?" Colby asked. "And look at that scar. Who did that?"

"I hope to find out this weekend, but someone has damaged her inside and out," Max responded in a quiet voice.

"I am here, Max. You don't have to deal with this alone," Colby said as he got up. He touched Max on the shoulder.

Max reached up and grabbed Colby's hand. "I know. Thanks for your help Colby. Love you queen."

"I am always here Max. Get some rest, Max. I love you too."

Max turned the lights out and slipped into bed.

Lying in the dark, Max listened to me breathe. Max wrapped her arms around me pulling me as close as possible.

"Max?" Sadie mumbled in her drunken sleep.

"I am here, Sadie. I am not going anywhere," Max replied.

12

"Later tonight. The wait will be worth
it,"
—Max

Max slid out of bed quietly so she wouldn't wake me. Looking over at me, Max leaned over and kissed me softly on the forehead. I grunted but fell back asleep. The clock was reading 8:30 am in the morning. Max slipped out of the bedroom quietly. Max joined Colby in the kitchen. Jumping on a bar stool, Max watched Colby pour her a cup of coffee.

"What time are you going to wake her, Max?"

"Probably about ten if she doesn't get up." Max blew the hot liquid in the cup before taking a sip.

Leaning on the countertop, Colby smiled at Max. "I love you, girl. Is everything good between you and Sadie? Something was going on with her, but I can't quite figure it out. She got her ass hammered last night and for what?"

"I really think she was nervous about the party or maybe about Zena being there. I really don't know why she would drink so much but that bitch Megan didn't help either," Max answered while looking at the bedroom door and back to Colby. "Colby, there is really something about Sadie that is so damned addicting. I just cannot get her out of my mind. I really like her. She makes me feel good about myself, which is something I never felt with Z."

Colby grabbed Max's hand. "You are falling for this girl."

"Maybe!" Max whispered. Then a smile came across her face. "Yeah, I am falling hard."

Colby tightened his grip on Max's hand. "You deserve to be in a happy relationship. Don't be scared to put yourself out there. Don't fight it, Max! I promise you; Tori, Lacey, Z and I are right here for you. Are you scared to open up to someone again?"

Max shrugged her shoulders, "I am a little scared."

"Are you taking your meds, Max, like you're supposed to?"

"Most of the time. The one pill makes me feel like I am in a fog and I hate that feeling, Colby. I really need to talk to the doctor about coming off those pills. I just hate them, and I do skip them every so often," Max finally admitted.

"Max, those pills are for keeping everything in check. We don't need you to lose control of your thoughts again. I can't handle you hurting yourself again. I can't lose you!"

"You won't, Colby. I promise you are stuck with me for the rest of our lives. I still want to talk to a doctor because I really think I am doing better." Max lifted off the seat and kissed Colby on the forehead. "Love you forever my queen!"

"Love you too but take your meds," Colby said sternly.

"Colby, I know you told Sadie about me trying to kill myself."

"Yes, I am sorry, Max. Please don't be mad at me."

"It is okay. Tori explained it all to me. I plan to tell her the whole story this weekend. I hope she will open up to me also. Somebody has really hurt her."

I shuffled in the bed. Her head thrashed side to side. Her legs kicked out. Small, light screams emerged as the nightmare was filling my dreams.

"Swallow the fucking pill!" he ordered. He pushed me hard against the wall. I couldn't breathe as he pushed me harder into the wall. In my brain, I was screaming *GET OFF!* His fingers tried to force my lips open. When he failed to separate my lips, he clamped down on my nose closing the nostrils causing the air to be cut off, frantically thrashing my head side to side before finally having no choice but to open my mouth or pass out. Parting my lips, I took a deep breath before I felt his fingers slip in. I tried to bite him, but that made him more enraged. "You are a fucking bitch!" he screamed. He kicked my legs out from under me, causing my body to hit the floor with a hard thump.

"Open your damn mouth. I will not ask you again!" He was leaning over me with his face filled with anger. So, I had to open my mouth letting him shove the pills inside. He held my mouth and nostrils closed at the same time to make me swallow. I just sat there defeated while waiting for the world to go fuzzy. This was his every weekend routine. He drugged me and then fucked me. The drugs made him feel more empowered. He didn't even realize it was not necessary because he was always in control.

Waking up slowly, I was naked on the bed with him on top. "Tell me you love me"! he ordered between the thrusting, his hand pressed over my mouth.

"I love you," mumbled out.

The words caused his thrusting to get harder. I watched him in the mirror as his ass moved up and down. His dick was large and filling me with cum. As he fucked me, pain would shoot through my vagina. His moaning was hard, and his breathing was in short breaths. "Take it bitch! Just take it!" he groaned out as he put his dick deeper inside releasing his nasty ass cum. He finally collapsed on top of me gasping for air. His body became dead weight once he emptied all his cum inside of me. Once his breathing eased, he finally rolled off me. I took a deep breath of air as the dead weight was gone.

Tears started rolling down my cheek.

I just don't know why I allowed this asshole to do this to me! I always thought this in the back of my mind.

He huffed then sat up on the side of the bed. "You are my wife. I own you bitch!"

I rolled over and curled into a ball. The physical abuse had been going on for about a year. He was always verbally abusive, but something just snapped in him. Maybe he was having trouble in the business, an empire he built from scratch, and he loved that business like his own child. If he was having trouble, I would be the last to know. He made it very clear to me that my place was at home and to give him a child, which I had not been able to do. Maybe that was where the anger was coming from.

He walked around the bed; he looked down at me then leaned

over. "You are my property, BITCH."

"Don't you fucking forget it? For life!"

It was now 10:10 am. Max just got out of the shower. Max quietly tiptoed into the room. Pulling a pair of jeans and shirt from the closet, she dressed while watching me sleep, my body lying halfway across the bed on my stomach with the sheets covering the mounds of my butt and the curves of the bare back glistening in the sunlight. Suddenly, I was kicking from under the sheets. Max crawled into bed laying a hand on my back. The kicking ceased, and I relaxed at Max's touch. Max leaned over and kissed my bare shoulder. "Sadie, you ready to wake up baby?" she whispered softly. I wiggled slightly.

"Hey! Try to open your eyes for me." Max softly rubbed my back.

I rolled over and stretched out before I opened one eye then closed it quickly. "Oh shit!" I frowned and then placed my arm over my eyes. What the hell did I do?

"You need water. Do you have a headache, Sadie?" Max asked in a gentle voice.

I shook my head weakly up and down. Max climbed over me making the bed move down with her weight. "Ugh!" I groaned. Max tried not to smile at my pain.

"Take these aspirin and drink some water." Max helped me sit up.

I was squinting my eyes. "I think I am dying here!"

"I think you will live. Want to go take a shower so we can head to the cabin?" Max asked as she rubbed my head.

"Oh, crap, Max! We should be gone by now." I laid back covering my eyes.

"As soon as you get going, we will get going. The cabin will be there when we get there," Max said in an assuring voice.

I threw my legs over the side of the bed. I had to sit there for the longest time with my head dropped.

Max finished getting ready before she returned to my side. Leaning over to Max, I used her body as a brace.

"I'm ready. Come on baby. Let's get me in the shower."

Max pulled me up to a standing position. "Do you need me to help you?" Max asked.

"I will be okay," I replied.

"You want some food?"

I shook my head no then I slipped into the shower. The warm water felt good. I just leaned against the wall letting the water rush over me. How in the hell did I let myself get so wasted last night? I remember three beers and two shots. Would that have been enough? Geesh…I was thinking; I must get myself together.

"I have a cooler to pack, so I will be right back to check on you," Max yelled out through the shower curtain. "Are you okay?"

"I am fine, Max. I will be out soon."

I finished letting the water hit me in the shower. I was sitting on the side of the bed when Max walked back into the bedroom. I was wrapped in a towel making little progress with getting dressed. "I can't find my clothes, Max."

"I put your bag in the closet."

Max went over and picked up my suitcase. "Are you sure you are okay? We can skip the cabin."

"No! We are going. Let me get dressed. Plus, you said the ride was two hours, so I am sure my body will feel better by then." I stood up and let the towel hit the floor. I wrapped my arms around Max's neck to steady myself. I reached down and grabbed Max's hand and placed it on my breast. Whispering in her ear, "I want your hand here tonight!" Max moaned and shifted herself to the words. I kissed Max's cheek then started to get dressed.

We entered the living room with our luggage. Colby greeted us. "*Hey,* you two! Ready for your weekend?" pulling a pair of sunglasses away from my eyes. "Oooooh, baby girl!" He placed the sunglasses back.

"Be safe, Colby. We will see you Monday afternoon," Max called out as she grabbed my wrist and led us out the door.

"Bye-bye girls!" Colby yelled out as the door closed.

Max headed the car out of town. The windows were down, but the air was a little humid. So, Max rolled the windows up turning on the air conditioner. That was all I needed. Within ten minutes I curled into a ball. With my sunglasses shielding me from the sun, I soon fell asleep. Before I fell asleep, I laid my hand on Max's thigh. It remained there until Max stopped at a diner about an hour into the ride.

Max leaned over and whispered into my ear. "Wake up Sadie. I need to eat and take my shot." Max rubbed my hair softly.

"I'm sorry, Max. Yes, of course." I sat up looking around the parking lot. We were in front of a diner. I was not as pale. The rosy color was slowly coming back into my cheeks. I felt more like a human.

Max pulled her shirt above her belly and injected the needle. Her face scrunched up in pain.

I reached over and rubbed the back of her neck to ease the pain, looking over at Max's belly, running my fingers gently over it. "You need to switch your shot site more often baby. You are making the stomach area really sensitive." I leaned over and kissed her belly before pulling the shirt down.

It was lunchtime, and the diner was almost full. We grabbed the last booth available. The server was a plump woman named Sheila, her uniform covered in spills of grease with a crooked name tag.

"What can I get you?" the server asked never looking up at us.

Max ordered a hamburger and fries, and I ordered a bowl of

soup. I figured it would be smart to eat something light. I sat back leaning my head against the booth. Last night was one big blur.

"Do I even want you to fill in the gaps from last night?" I asked Max reluctantly.

Max looked at me for the longest time before she spoke. "Why did you drink so much?"

"I don't know. I haven't done that in a very long time. I just started, and I couldn't stop. I am sorry, Max! I must have embarrassed you in front of your friends."

"I wasn't embarrassed. I don't really care what my friends think. I am sure you would have been embarrassed though," Max said.

"Oh my God, Max! What happen?" I sat straight up. I was thinking for a second. "What the hell. "Was I naked?"

"Very much so," Max answered.

"Oh my, your friends saw me naked. They saw my scar?" I just buried my face.

"Yes, but no one has asked about it except Colby." Max reached out and grabbed my hand. "Don't worry about it."

"Right. Don't worry!" I just lowered my head shaking it. I looked back up at Max. "Did I tell you Zena had a penis?"

Just then, Sheila, the server, brought the food over to the table and sat it down. Max held her face down and smiled. Sheila shook her head as she walked away.

"Yes, but I am not sure what that was about." Max was rubbing my hand. "This girl named Megan fed you laced brownies with hash in them. I figured maybe you were seeing things."

"No, no, I saw Zena having sex with that girl she brought to the party. She had a penis on and was…well you know what she was doing." I looked around to see if anyone else heard me.

Max got quiet for a moment. "It's fine, Sadie. Let's stop thinking about last night and enjoy our trip. Now, eat your soup before it gets cold. Having something hot in your stomach will do you good."

Once we finished eating, we continued our trip to the cabin. With every hill and dip on the drive my stomach did flips, and with every curve, my head swirled. I just stayed quiet. I didn't want to bring up last night anymore. Max told me we would stop in town to pick up a few things. The town was located about four miles from the cabin. It was very small with a grocery store, gas station, one restaurant and a bar. We pulled into the gas station to fill the car up. The pumps were old, and the gas station itself was ancient. Max jumped out to go pay, and I decided to get out and stretch my legs. A pickup truck pulled on the other side of the pumps, and two men jumped out.

"Hi!" I said.

"Hey, sexy. Are you looking for a date?" the man with a beer belly said.

I quickly got back in the car, locking the doors behind me. The man stared at me while he pumped his gas. A few times, he rubbed his private area. Max walked out of the gas station. Passing the beer belly man she just nodded. Max pumped the gas then tried to get in the car, but the door was locked.

"Open the door, Sadie!" Max jumped in. "You okay?"

"Yes. I must have locked the door by accident."

"Next stop is the grocery store, then to the cabin," Max said as she smiled over at me. I smiled back softly sitting back in the seat. I stayed in the car as Max went into the grocery store. She wasn't gone but a few minutes and then came back out with a bag of groceries. Jumping in the car, Max smiled and rubbed my hair. I smiled back and watched as she drove the car through the hills.

Max pulled the car into the driveway of the cabin. I looked out the windshield at the gorgeous structure. The cabin looked like it belonged in a magazine. Max opened the front door, and the entryway opened into a huge living room with a fireplace. Just past the living room were French doors that looked out to the lake. It was just beautiful, peaceful scenery. Upstairs was a loft with a few bedrooms.

"Whose place is this, Max?" I asked as I ran my fingers over the couch. "It is beautiful." Spinning around I was admiring the structure.

"It is mine, Sadie. Tori helped me build it about five years ago." Max wrapped her arms around me. "Lacey helped me get the land for a great deal. It is a work in progress."

I turned to Max, wrapping my arms around Max's neck, kissing her softly. Our lips were wetting each other's, our tongues slipping in and out slowly, Max's hands touching my hip then slipping up my back. I moaned into her mouth, causing Max to pull away.

"Everything okay?" I asked.

Brushing the hair from my face, she said, "Not now, baby." Max nibbled on my ear. I moaned again. "Later tonight. The wait will be worth it," Max whispered.

13

"I love you, Sadie!"
—Max

"I love you too, Max!"
—Sadie

The sky was dark and filled with sparkling stars. The fire brightened the air with little flames that escaped then floated upward. The slightest chill was in the air with the silhouette of the mountains in the distance.

Max and I were relaxing in an oversized hammock by the fire, wrapped in a blanket with our bodies intertwined, half full glasses of wine beside us. We were just lying here for the longest time in silence listening to the sounds of nature every so often trying to guess the animal that was behind the noise.

Max finally broke the silence.

"Sadie, can we talk?" Max asked as she slipped a piece of hair behind my ear. "I want to tell you about Zena. I know Colby talked to you, but I want you to hear and know it all from me."

I just nodded yes and sat there in silence. Max interlaced her fingers with mine.

"Let me start off by saying, I really didn't want to tell you everything, Sadie. Not because I want to lie to you, it is just hard for me to open up." Max took a deep breath. "And it is embarrassing."

"Talk to me, Max," I whispered as she rubbed the top of my hand.

"Zena and I were together for a few years like I told you. She cheated on me, and it broke my heart. What Z did just destroyed me. I was in love with her, but I can promise you, Sadie, that is in the past." I noticed Max's breathing was increasing and her breaths were becoming short.

"Max, I need you to take a deep breath." I laid her hand on my chest so she could feel my breath. Just take a deep breath with me, Max, and try to relax.

Max exhaled slowly.

"Do it again for me. Take your time," I whispered in her ear.

"I stopped eating, going out and talking to my friends. Everything was just eating me up inside. I couldn't let things go. Z was the only woman I had ever loved in my life. I guess I couldn't find a way to work it out in my head. Then one day…" Max got quiet.

"Let me feel you take another breath, Max." I waited to feel Max exhale.

"Then one day, I came home from work, got in the tub and I took a bottle of sleeping pills. It seemed like that was my only choice to get relief from the misery. I was close to death when Colby found me. I was on life support for five days in the hospital." Max wiped a tear away. "I knew I hurt all my friends because I couldn't deal," Max whispered between tears. "I still have to take pills to help me deal with things."

I turned to Max's tear-stained face and kissed her softly, wiping tears from her cheek. "Max, tell me the rest," I said softly.

"The rest?" Max asked tentatively.

"Yes. Why did Zena cheat on you? What upset you so bad that you would try to take your life? It wasn't because a woman cheated on you. I have known you for a few weeks, and I know you are too strong to let someone cheating on you cause a suicide attempt. Maybe that is what you told everyone else, but I am not buying it." I planted a small peck on Max's cheek letting my lips linger. "I am here, Max. I am right here, and I am not going anywhere!"

Max reached into her pocket and pulled out a pill bottle; she fumbled with the lid until I took it away. Reading the bottle, I noticed it was for anxiety. I placed it on the table beside the hammock.

"Max, take a breath. You don't need those pills right now. If you need them after we talk, you can have them. Look at me, Max! You are okay."

"That is just it, Sadie. I am not okay. Tori, Lacey, Colby and even Zena don't know the whole story. I have never told a soul, not even my doctors." Max threw her head back closing her eyes. I rubbed her forehead waiting for her to continue. "You know I don't like…" Max just faded off.

"Go ahead, baby," I whispered.

"Zena cheated on me because she was never able to be inside of me nor could she touch me down there. I imagine she wanted more and that other woman gave it to her. I can't blame her for that. It was not fair to deny someone that pleasure. I wouldn't be surprised if you don't get annoyed with it eventually and need something I may never be able to give you."

"That will never happen, Max." I looked into Max's eyes feeling her pain. I whispered again, "Never!" Max was starting to shake. I wrapped her in the blanket. "Now, tell me, what made you swallow the pills?"

Max took a huge breath followed by a long pause. "Zena and I went to a party, and we were drinking. When we got home, Z was very aggressive with me. It was the alcohol that made Z shove her hand down there. I freaked out tossing her off the bed. Her head hit the chair knocking her out. "I could have killed her." Max started to tear up again. "Z forcing her way between my legs brought back bad memories. I found out about the other woman a few days later. It snowballed. We broke up, and my memories wouldn't leave me alone. They just flooded my mind."

"Tell me why no one can touch you in that way, Max?"

Max's voice was weak. "I have never told anyone that, Sadie."

"Maybe you need to talk about it to someone. If not me maybe someone like Colby?"

"NO! NO! Sadie." The tears started to stream down Max's cheek again.

"Okay, baby!" I was starting to tear up.

There was silence again. Then Max tried to speak.

"When I was fourteen or maybe fifteen, I was…" Max started to hyperventilate.

I placed my hand on Max's chest and looked into her eyes, her face inches from mine. "Look at me, Max. Breathe with me. In now and out, that's good, baby. Keep doing it with me. Feel better?"

"I am trying, Sadie."

"I know. I know...Max."

Max closed her eyes and exhaled. She opened her eyes and looked at me with tears running from her eyes.

"I was fifteen and headed to see Colby for the summer. His father and his friend came to Texas to pick me up. That was where my family moved to, which separated Colby and me, but I would visit in the summer. We stopped at a hotel about halfway. I couldn't wait to see Colby that summer. Actually, I had a girlfriend back home. I couldn't wait to tell Colby about her. I was asleep when the two men came back from the bar." Max paused for the longest time. Then she broke down crying.

My thoughts exploded in my head as I listen to her words. In my mind, I was thinking, OH SHIT I know where this is going.

Between her heaves of cries, I barely heard her say it for the first time in her life. "They! They!" Max crying increased. "I couldn't stop them.... I tried but I couldn't.... They... they—raped me. Colby's father raped me."

I pulled Max into a tight embrace. "Okay baby, it's okay! Keep breathing for me." I started to rock with Max. I just held her tight for almost thirty minutes allowing her to just cry it all out. Max's cries started to slow down, and she could speak again.

"I said it. It is out, but Colby doesn't know. You must promise to never say anything. You can't say anything to him, Sadie, PLEASE!" Max was pleading in a panic.

"I will NEVER repeat what you just shared," I replied while trying to keep her calm and comfort her. I opened the bottle of pills and handed Max one pill with her glass of wine. "Do you need to check your sugar, baby?"

"No, my sugar is fine." Max swallowed the pill with a sip of wine. Handing the glass back to me, she laid her head on my chest.

"Sadie?"

, Max."

"I am falling in love with you," Max whispered softly.

"Me too, baby," I whispered back softly.

Wrapped in each other's arms, we just laid there quietly until both fell asleep. The fire was starting to burn down when Max opened her eyes. I was still asleep when Max reached up and cupped my face. My eyes fluttered open. "Everything okay?" I asked.

"Yes, baby!" I let our lips touch softly then whispered over them, "I want to make love to you. Follow me." Max grabbed my wrist pulling me out of the hammock. Max walked me inside then suddenly I stopped in my tracks.

Max turned around. "Something wrong?"

"No. I just need a moment. I will be right back."

"I am going to start a fire. I will be right here waiting on you."

The fire was roaring, and the glow was lighting the room. Huge furry blankets covered the floor. Candles were lit, and the smell of lilac floated in the air. Max turned her head when she heard steps from behind. Turning completely around, she got the first glance of me standing in front of her in an opal, white-laced gown attached to every curve of my body as the material flowed to the floor, small lace straps holding it up, my breast trying to burst out free.

"Wow!" Max stepped closer. "Put your hands behind your back." Max reached behind grabbing my wrists, her mouth sucking softly in the crook of my neck. Max placed her free hand on my breast. Max rolled her palm over the hard nipple.

"You look amazing. You are so beautiful, Sadie. I want to smother you with love."

"Kneel!" Max said as she freed my arms. I obeyed and kneeled. Max lowered herself down with me.

Max pulled the gown straps down revealing my breasts. Max placed my arms around her neck, then wet her fingers before her fingers playing with my hard nipples. Pulling my nipples, she twisted softly causing me to lay my head back in a long moan.

"Tell me what you want, Sadie!"

"You!" I whispered.

Max pulled the gown over my head." Lie down, baby!" Max helped me lie back softly.

Max kneeled above me pulling her shirt off revealing her undone jean button. Her bra was tight and filled with breasts. Laying on me, our skin touching, Max's fingers scraped over my skin as she pulled my leg up over her thigh.

"Max!" I moaned out.

"You turn me on when you say my name," Max said through her moan as her lips sucked on my neck.

I reached up and unlatched Max's bra, slipping it off, then letting it fall to the floor. Max released her ponytail letting the strands of hair fall over her breasts. I swallowed hard as I felt my vagina tighten. Max unzipped the jeans revealing the top of her mound.

"I am going to lay down, and I want you to undress the rest of me. Be careful where you touch me, Sadie. *You understand?*"

"I understand."

Max laid down and rolled me on top. I kneeled between Max's legs. Max lifted her ass when I slipped the jeans down tossing them to the side then lifting again when I pulled down her panties letting them join the jeans. I bent over letting my mouth kiss her stomach, stopping to lick around Max's belly button, my hand softly grasping at her left breast. Max laid a hand on my head wanting my lips to linger. She watched as my tongue dipped into her belly button then licked slowly around.

Max tossed her head back. "That feels damn good!" Her breathing was becoming heavier.

We rolled over, so I was back on the bottom. Max lowered her head and rolled her tongue around my stiffened nipple, licking and sucking eagerly on the nipple as it responded becoming harder. I arched up into her mouth. Max let the nipple fall from her mouth, her mouth traveling back up finding my lips, our tongues licking at each other. Max softly bit my lower lip.

"Sadie! I want to taste you!"

"Max, you mean…?"

"Yes! I want my mouth on your pussy."

"Um.…what if I? You know…"

Max pulled away looking in my eyes with a smile. "It will be okay if that happens."

"No one has ever… I have never …" I said nervously.

Max smiled then kissed down my neck slowly again sucking gently as her hand ran over my thigh, her mouth moving back up letting her hungry tongue slip between my lips. Our tongues deep in passion twirls, Max's hand traveled up rolling over the hardened nipples.

I moaned out exciting Max.

"Let me taste you!" Max was breathing hard.

I released a small gasp, "Yes."

Max nibbled on my ear whispering, "You have me wet as hell, and I'm ready to make love to you."

Max kissed her way over my breasts then worked down to my thighs before spreading my legs. Her mouth covered the top of the bare mound with small kisses. Max took her fingers and spread my lips wide open exposing my vagina. Max studied my vagina for a moment before her face lowered. Licking softly over my clit in small circles, I gasped aloud and arched with my hands clawing at the blankets, her tongue slipping in and out of my pussy then back around the clit, sucking gently making it swollen. Juices escaped from inside of me. Max licked in long strokes. Max pulled away. I am going to cum too fast. It was feeling so good, and I have not had anything to make me feel this good, in this way.

I was breathing hard. "Max, please don't stop."

Max lowered her head again sucking hard on the clit, her hands on the inside of my thighs holding both legs apart. She felt my hand come down on her head as she slipped her tongue inside. It was warm and wet causing Max to moan deep inside of me. Max's pussy was releasing juices. She rolled her tongue around my pussy finding the love spot. She stroked it with her tongue a few times before I felt myself tense and raise my ass up.

"Oh my God, Max!" I could feel a climax quickly reaching its peak causing me to scream out. Her tongue in my pussy was feeling so good. I did not want to cum too quickly. I couldn't stop. The climax was starting to end when Max slipped her tongue out replacing it with her finger. Even Max's finger in my pussy had me soaking wet. I groaned hard as I felt Max's finger, then her mouth back on my pussy. A sucking noise could be heard as Max ate hungrily. Max continued to slip her finger in and out slowly. My pussy was wet as hell. I was really enjoying her tongue and finger. I could enjoy this ALL the time!

"OH! … BABY! …" I arched hard and twisted as I exploded again into Max's mouth and all over her finger. Gasping as the explosion ended, my ass lowered back down to the soft rugs. Max slipped out of me slowly before kissing upward over my body. I released little moans after climaxing several times.

Max rolled over to the side turning me toward her. I let my fingers stroll over Max's hard nipples. Closing her eyes, Max breathed in.

I leaned over kissing her. "I can taste myself," I said between the kiss.

Max moaned hard into the kiss.

"Show me a limit, baby!" I said.

Max rolled to her back letting her pussy be exposed.

"Promise you will stop if I ask?"

"Yes, I will stop."

Max placed my hand on top of hers. She took in a deep breath. "Don't move your hand from the top of mine." I watched as Max placed our hands on herself. I made sure I kept my hand still. Max was rubbing up and down slow and soft with my hand mirroring.

"Max!" I said softly as I watched our hands on Max. I could sense Max was tense.

I whispered in her ear, "Can I talk to you, baby?"

"Please!"

I leaned over to Max's ear. "Your mouth made my pussy so wet."

"Ah…" Max gasped out.

"Are you wet, Max?"

"Yes." Her breathing increased, and her strokes became longer.

"Touch my nipple, Max, and pinch it," I groaned out as Max's finger pinched down hard.

Max moaned when she heard me moan. Her hand was pushing in and out of her pussy. She was inside.

I am going to suck on your nipples. Will you watch me?" I whispered over her lips.

"AH! … Yes, Sadie!"

My lips pulled Max's nipple out until it was hard and erect. I began sucking softly on the nipples. Max's eyes watched my mouth devour her. Max's breathing was in short gasps as her finger was still moving in and out of her pussy slowly but not forcing the thrust. She slipped out every so often to roll around her clit before she eased the finger back in.

"Sadie!" Max was starting to arch.

I slipped up and pressed my mouth to Max's lips. Mouthing the words, "I want you to cum for me."

Max stopped the soft thrusting letting her finger fill her as she exploded. The juices touched my hand causing me to moan out. Max's whole body jerked as she started to cum. Her body lowered back down. We were kissing softly now when I whispered out in desire.

"Slip your finger out!"

Max obeyed moaning as her wet finger slipped out. I guided Max's hand.

"Slip it in me, Max."

The feel of the juices mixing was so arousing to Max. Squeezing her legs together, Max closed her eyes and groaned out, "I am cumming again...!"

I arched releasing myself just as hard for the third time.

Both exhausted as our explosions came to an end, we just collapsed into each other arms.

"I love you, Sadie!"

"I love you too, Max!"

We laid together in each other's arms. I looked into the fire thinking I was going to have to tell Max my story soon.

The sand was starting to fall.

14

"Sadie! Do you want to tell me?"
—Max

The morning sun was shining brightly through the bedroom window. Max was lying on her belly sleeping hard. The amazing lovemaking and her releasing those words that she has never spoken before has worn her out. Her bare back was exposed with her hair flowing downward toward her butt. Max was more than beautiful. She was gorgeous. Every curve of her body was enticing and perfect. Looking at her body just made me wet. I was sitting here watching her sleep trying my best to figure it all out. Why did Max love me? I held my own in looks but nothing compared to Max. I looked like an elementary teacher whereas Max was more like the local news lady.

I slipped quietly out of bed trying not to wake Max. I put on a pair of sweatpants and a hoodie and tiptoed out of the bedroom. Walking inside of the living room, I glanced over at the pile of disarray blankets. My mind went racing back to the night before, Max's touch and mouth all over me. She even kissed my scar. She loved all of me. I felt a twitch in my vagina again as my mind filled with thoughts. I folded the blankets and picked up the wine glasses, taking them to the sink. Looking out the window, the sun was appearing over the mountains. A low fog hovered over the water on the lake.

I walked down to the lake to take the view in and to think. The dew still covered the grass making it moist to the touch. I curled up in the beach chair at the end of the pier. I watched the fog slowly move over the water, seeing it disappear when it met another object, sitting there with my legs pulled up, my arms wrapped around them thinking about Max and what she told me the night before. I could imagine those men holding her down and forcing themselves on her. No one could hear her muffled screams, no one to help her. How she held the story in for so many years unable to speak of it was unimaginable. Max let it eat her up like acid on the inside for so long. It was so bad that she would try to take her own life. I wanted so much to erase her pain. I wiped a tear away. My thoughts shifted to my own life. How was I going to tell Max about my marriage and what I had been through? Would Max still want to be in my life?

I was deep in thought when I felt Max slip in behind me on the chair. Handing me a cup of coffee, Max pulled me back letting me lean on her.

"Hey!"

"Hey, you!" I leaned my head back and kissed Max's cheek.

"The fog is beautiful this morning," Max said as she sipped her coffee. "And so are you!"

"Yes, it is peaceful."

"What have you been doing down here?"

"Mostly thinking."

"About?"

"Mostly about what you told me last night, thinking about the pain you went through alone. Thinking of a way I could help you to stop the pain." I said as I stared into the fog.

Max wrapped her arm around my waist then whispered. "Your hand on mine between my legs last night was the closest I have ever come to letting anybody touch me down there. There is something about you that opens me up the way no one has ever done before. You are helping with my pain."

"Thank you for letting me in, Max. Baby, have you ever had a woman's exam?" I asked.

"No"

Now, that isn't good.

"I can't. You said you were mostly thinking about what I told you last night. What else were you thinking about?"

I took a deep breath in then let it out. I closed my eyes, and the silence was deafening for a while.

"Sadie! Do you want to tell me?"

I lowered my head and shook it yes. "I am afraid I will lose you."

"That is not going to happen. You haven't run because of my story, and I will not run because of yours. I promise you, Sadie."

I breathed in again, and it became shallow and rapid as I tried to start the story. "I…I…um…I… Damn it!"

Max tighten her grip around my waist pulling me closer. "Take your time."

"I am from upstate New York. Born and raised with my whole family there and a…" I exhaled slowly, "and a husband." Again, I exhaled, "I married my high school boyfriend right out of school. He has always been verbally abusive, but the last year before I left him he became physical."

I closed my eyes and leaned my head back. Max didn't say a word, but I felt a kiss on my temple.

"I couldn't take it anymore, so I ran." I started to tear up. "He is an evil man. If he ever finds me…" My words faded off and were replaced with sniffles.

Max wrapped both her arms around me. I lowered my head as if I had something to be ashamed of.

Max whispered in my ear, "What did he do to you?"

Heaves just started. "He beat me, force fucked me and locked me in closets. I always lived in fear Max and I still am.…"

Max was trying to control her temper. This had always been a challenge when someone she cared about got hurt. "Did the beatings cause that scar?"

"Yes!" barely slipped through my lips. "I did something he didn't like, and he cut me with a hacksaw. He tied my arms and legs to a saw table then he cut me with the saw while I was stretched out." I just burst out in tears. I covered my face and whispered, "He didn't want anyone to know so he wouldn't take me to the hospital. Instead, a doctor came to the house and sewed me up there with no anesthesia."

"Oh my God, baby." Max just went into a daze after listening. Fury was building up inside of her.

I tried to break free and run from Max.

Max wrapped me up in her legs. "Don't pull away, baby. I am right here."

I struggled for a moment before I collapsed in Max's arms crying. "You are safe now Sadie."

I whispered into her chest, "I haven't seen my family for months because of fear. I miss them so much. They hired a lawyer trying to get me a divorce, but I don't know what is going on. I am afraid to call. I am sorry to get you involved in my mess, Max. I can understand if you don't want to be with me.

"You didn't do anything wrong, Sadie. I want to be with you forever." Max rubbed my head softly. "That son of a bitch needs to get what is coming to him." Max was angry but trying her best not to show it. "This can be fixed baby. We can fix this. I want you in my life. He won't ever hurt you again."

"I want to be in your life too, but even if I get a divorce, he will not let me go. He never will. He'd rather see me dead." Suddenly, I started to panic. "He will hurt you or your friends. I can't do this to you. No, Max! Let me go!"

I was fighting Max at this point to free myself. Both coffee cups toppled over shattering on the pier. The sound caused me to stop fighting. The vision of the shattered glass sliding across the kitchen floor surfaced. My eyes closed and I collapsed backward into Max's arms.

❧

"Sadie, Sadie, open your eyes for me." Max had carried me from the pier to the bedroom. Max sat next to me wiping my forehead with a cool towel.

I slowly opened my eyes.

"Hey!" Max looked down smiling.

"Hey, you!" I looked up smiling back.

Her smile disappeared as she started to panic again.

"No baby, look at me. You believe in me? You believe in us?" Max asked while she held both my wrists.

I looked at Max's fingers wrapped around my wrist and whispered, "I do. But ... But—"

"But nothing, baby. We will fix both of us, and we will do it together." Max leaned over kissing me gently. I started to melt into the kiss and finally relax.

"It will be okay, baby. I promise you. You have me now to help you through this."

"I really need to stop passing out on you." I smiled.

"You do. Do you know how heavy you are?"

"Hey." I punched Max in the arm.

"I have some steaks thawed. Thought we would grill them for lunch then go into town for a few supplies and maybe some ice cream." Max smiled down at me.

"That sounds great but baby it is only nine in the morning." I pointed toward the clock sitting beside the bed.

Max leaned over smiling. "Then we just need to occupy the next three hours. What would you suggest, Ms. Sadie?" Max pulled at the strings of my hoodie.

"We need to occupy three hours. That may be a little long, especially for you." I smiled.

"Oh, I see." Max lowered her body over mine. "Then I think I'm up for a challenge."

Passion, love and laughter filled the next few hours. The past was now placed on a shelf for the time being. Three hours went by fast. Then, before I knew it, I was in the shower while Max headed out to the grill.

I stepped out of the shower, wrapped a towel around me and headed to the bedroom to get dressed. I dropped the towel to the floor and looking at the scar in the mirror. Maxine loved me with all my scars. I looked down and ran my finger along the ragged skin. Looking back up in the mirror, I screamed.

"FUCK! MAX! MAX!" I reached down and grabbed the towel off the floor. I ran toward the bedroom door when Max ran through it almost falling to the floor as our bodies collided.

"Jesus, what is the matter?" Max was trying to keep her balance.

"There is a man looking in the window," I pointed at the open window across the room.

"What?"

Max walked over to the window. Leaning over, she looked out. "Tommy, what the hell are you doing. Go to the side door." Max started to head out.

"Come on out after you get dressed." Max closed the door behind her.

I looked in the mirror while thinking, "Who the hell is Tommy?"

❧

I walked out and found Max and this young man on the patio. Max was flipping the steaks on the grill. The young man was sitting at the table drinking a Coke.

"I am starving, and it smells terrific," I said aloud to announce my presence.

"Hey!" Max came over and kissed me on the cheek. I moved backward and nodded my head toward the young man sitting at the table.

"No worry. Sadie, this is Tommy, and he knows, don't you Tommy?"

"Tommy knows Max likes women."

"What do you have to say to Ms. Sadie?"

"Sorry I looked in the window," Tommy said in a low voice. "That wasn't the right thing to do."

"Tommy helps me with the upkeep of the cabin when I am not

here, Max explained. He does a great job. His family lives down the road. He is a good kid."

"Yep, a good kid!" Tommy repeated.

I sat down at the table with him. "Well, Tommy, a friend of Max is a friend of mine. So, Tommy, do you want to share my steak with me and stay for lunch?" I asked the young man.

Max smiled at me.

Tommy became excited. "Yes, I will stay for lunch. Can Tommy get another Coke?"

"Of course, Tommy, in the fridge and bring me and Sadie a water please."

"Okay." Tommy stood up and went inside.

Max turned to me. "That is nice to invite him. He has Asperger's."

"He seems to be very nice. I started college because I always wanted to work with special needs children in some capacity. Of course, Brad didn't approve, and he made me be a trophy housewife instead... Brad is my husband's name. I don't think I told you that earlier."

"I will just call him asshole or bastard if that is okay with you," Max said as she turned the grill off.

"Got the water, Max!" Tommy was coming through the patio doors.

We sat there eating the steaks with fried corn on the cob and baked potatoes. The three of us sat there laughing while we filled our bellies.

"I didn't know you could cook, Max," I said as I placed my fork on the plate and leaned back in the chair.

"I can grill better than I cook," Max replied.

Tommy looked at his watch. "Tommy has to go cut grass now," he said as he stood up. "Thanks for the food, Max and Ms. Sadie." He held his fist out for fist pumps.

"Nice to meet you, Tommy."

"Max?" Tommy said as he started to walk.

"Yes, Tommy?" Max answered.

"Ms. Sadie has nice tits." He laughed as he walked away.

Max just smiled at Sadie. "Yes, she does, Tommy! Very nice tits."

I mouthed silently, Oh my God!

Max wanted to help clean up, but I insisted she go take a shower and I could do the dishes.

Max lowered her head in the shower allowing the water to pound the back of her neck. Unable to stop the tears, she let her emotions overcome her. Speaking of her past was hard enough but listening to Sadie's story overwhelmed her. She thought of all the ways she would hurt that bastard. She lifted her head and let the water wash away her tears. What Sadie had endured was unthinkable. Max slammed her fist on the shower wall.

I finished the dishes just as Max walked into the kitchen. I turned around to face her wrapping Max in a hug.

"You smell good," I whispered in her ear.

"You feel good," Max whispered back. "Ready to go to the town?"

"I am ready to go anywhere with you Maxine Shields."

15

"There is always time for a new beginning,"
—Sadie

Max pulled the car in front of the grocery store. We jumped out and headed in to grab a few items. Two men were sitting on the porch by the front door of the store. One of the men I recognized from the other day. It was the rude man from the gas pumps at the service station. Max was in front of me going into the store when the guy stuck his leg up blocking the door entrance.

"Move your leg!" Max ordered. Then Max repeated, "Move your fucking leg!"

"Maxine, hey little girl! I haven't seen you in such a long time. An elderly gray-headed lady stepped from inside the store. "Get that leg down, Frank!" The elderly lady swatted at the man's leg with a broom.

"Hey, Mrs. Tolbert. It has been over a year. How are you?" Max grabbed my wrist and walked into the store.

"I am just fine. Who is your friend?" Mrs. Tolbert asked.

"This is Sadie, Mrs. Tolbert. Sadie, this is Mrs. Tolbert. She owns the store."

"Afternoon ma'am, nice to meet you!"

"Nice to meet you, young lady. What are you looking for today Maxine?" Ms. Tolbert asked as she walked behind the counter.

"Need some bread and a few more items," Max replied.

Max gathered the items and paid while I was looking around the store.

Finally, I finished looking around and took my one item to the counter. "I would like to buy this!"

"An hourglass, Sadie?" Max said.

I flipped it over, and the sand started to fall. "There is always time for a new beginning," I said as I flipped the hourglass over again. "See!"

Max smiled, and we said goodbye to Mrs. Tolbert after I paid for the hourglass. We exited the store to find Frank sitting on the hood of Max's car.

"Take the groceries and get in the car, Sadie," Max ordered

putting herself between me and Frank.

Frank just sat there smoking a cigarette and watching Sadie, get in the car. Max closed the door behind me and walked around to the back of the car to the driver side and jumped in. Frank stood up and turned around watching us pull away tossing his cigarette butt toward the car.

"Asshole!" Max said as we pulled off.

"What is his problem?" I asked Max.

"I don't know, but it is not our problem. Do you feel like ice cream, Sadie?"

"Sure, Max, that sounds good!"

Max drove for about two miles down the road to an ice cream parlor called Xan's. It was a small building but always stayed busy because people came from miles away for the homemade ice cream.

I got a single scoop of rocky road and Max got a sugar-free vanilla. We sat at a table in the corner enjoying the creamy ice cream.

I had to tell Max sugar-free ice cream could still raise her glucose.

"Yes mom, but I am careful. Been dealing with diabetes since I was seven." Max smiled.

"I just worry about you, baby."

Max grabbed her chair and pulled it closer. "I know." she leaned over and kissed my cheek softly.

"Sadie, I have something for you."

"For me?"

Max placed a box on the table. "It is a disposable cell phone. It is untraceable. I got it back at the store. Call your family Sadie."

I sat there staring at the box. My eyes were filling with tears. With every blink, a tear rolled down my cheek.

"It is safe, Sadie. We are two hours from where we live, in the mountains, and it is a disposable phone. Call them, Sadie!"

Max opened the box and placed the battery in the phone

turning it on. Then she sat it down in front of me.

Reaching out with shaking hands I touched the phone.

"Look at me, Sadie!"

I lifted my red eyes to Max's eyes. "Call them!"

Slowly, I picked the phone up, holding it for a few seconds.

"I'm scared" I whispered.

"I am right here," Max said as her hand laid on my thigh.

Slowly, my fingers started to push down the numbers. With one final hesitant stroke, I hit the send button.

Ring!

Ring!

Ring!

"Hello!" the female on the other end answered.

"Hello!" she repeated.

I didn't say anything until Max squeezed my thigh.

"Patsy?"

"OH, MY GOD! Where are you?" the woman asked.

I am safe. How is Mom?"

"She is fine but worried. She is here with me. He was sent the divorce papers a few days ago. He is really pissed off. The court date is set for the 24th of next month. You have to be there!"

"I just don't know if I can, Patsy. I can't talk long, but I will call you back soon. Put mom on the phone. I love you, sis!"

"Hello" the older woman's voice came through the phone.

"I love you, Mom!" I blurted out crying.

"Come home! Please come home!" the older woman pleaded.

"Not right now Mom, but I will soon. It is still too dangerous."

"I love you, baby girl. I didn't know what was happening to you."

"I know you didn't, Mom. I love you. I must go, Mom. It may not be safe to stay long on the phone."

With tears in my eyes, I reached down and hit end to disconnect the call. Sitting there looking at the phone in my unsteady hand, I broke down. Max reached over and guided me to her lap. She wrapped her arms around me softly, taking the phone from my hand laying it on the table. She reached up and placed my head on her shoulder.

"It is okay to cry, baby. Let it out." Max held me tight.

When the tears started to ease, I whispered softly, "Thank you."

Max whispered back "What did they tell you?"

"He was served the divorce papers. He isn't happy, and the court date is next month on the twenty-fourth, and I need to be there."

"Then we will figure a way to get you there."

"I don't see how," I said as I buried my face into Max's neck.

"Tell me about your family, Sadie," Max asked trying to lighten the topic.

"I have one sister and my mom. My dad passed in 2005 from cancer. My mom and sister will like you."

The truck door slammed loudly, and men's voices could be heard across the parking lot. It was Frank and a few other guys. They were drinking beer, being loud and obnoxious. It didn't take Frank long to notice us sitting in the corner. He headed over toward us screaming.

"Look, guys, we have two dykes here!"

Max leaned over and whispered to me; "Don't let them grab you. If they get you, I may not be able to do anything." Max grabbed my wrist standing me up and placing me behind her.

"Hey! Y'all two dykes need a big dick to show you how to be girls." He grabbed at his dirty dick through his pants.

"Go away Frank and let us be!" Max yelled out.

"Come here!" Frank yelled as he pretended to charge at Max. He laughed when Max jumped backward.

The other two guys were staying back. They seem like they really didn't want to get involved. Max let go of my hand and stepped forward, "Back the fuck off and go sober up!" she told Frank.

"You must be the man. Okay, want to be the man, show me your balls." Frank yelled. Frank jumped toward Max, and she stepped to the side quickly, crouching down as Frank stumbled past her. He stood up and gathered himself before turning toward Max again. His fists came up, and he headed toward her causing Max to bend her knees in a stance.

Frank laughed, "Look at this bitch!"

He swung at Max with a right hand, Max ducked and came up with her right foot into his ribs. Frank doubled over before coming up with a left hook. Max dipped and swept his legs from underneath him. He hit the ground with a big ass thump.

"Back off, Frank, before someone gets hurt!" Max yelled out.

"Fucking BITCH!" Frank yelled as he came to his feet.

Frank charged Max. She stepped to the side, and Frank hit the ground again sliding on his big ass beer belly like he was on a sled. He stood up wiping the dirt off.

The two other guys and I stayed away from the fight. That was good for Max. She didn't have to worry about my wellbeing.

Frank came toward Max again, but this time he got ahold of Max's right arm. He hit Max across the face hard. I heard his fist hit Max's face from where I was standing. Max went down on one knee in pain.

"Max!" I stepped toward her.

Max held her hand up to stop me from moving toward her. Max closed her fist and brought her hand up between his legs. Frank doubled over in agony, letting go of Max's arm. He grabbed his manhood as he gasped for air. Max jumped up grabbing his head and jamming her knee into his face. Frank fell back hitting the dirt; he was semiconscious laying stretch out moaning in pain. The two guys moved toward Max. She went into another stance as she readied herself to take them on. The two guys held their hands up in defensive positions. They leaned over picking up Frank and carried him to the truck. They threw him in the back of the truck bed and took off.

I was standing there with my jaw dropped. Max ran over to me. "You Okay?"

"Am I okay? Am I okay? Are you fucking kidding me right now? What the hell is that? You just kicked that man's ass!"

"Ouch! Don't make me laugh." Max held her cheek.

"Let me see," I ordered. "It is already starting to swell. We need to put some ice on it."

I walked over to the window and asked for some ice from the lady behind the counter.

"Your girlfriend is hot and a badass!" The lady said as she handed the ice out the window.

"Yes, she is." I smiled as I grabbed the ice.

Kissing Max cheek, I placed ice on the red area. Max winced when the ice touched her face.

"So...?" I said.

"I am a black belt, and so is Tori," Maxi replied.

"Oh, that's nothing I need to know!" I said sarcastically.

"Now you do." Max smiled then winced again.

"You keep amazing me all the time. I keep falling deeper in love with you," I whispered over Max's lips before I kissed her. I told Max I would drive back as I grabbed her wrist.

"Oh, now you grab my wrist. I don't think so!" Max switched the hands grabbing my wrist leading me to the car.

Going back through the mountains headed for the cabin, Max laid her head back letting the ice cool her throbbing face. I reached over and rubbed her head. Max's eyes were closed. "You okay, baby?" I asked. "Baby? Hey Max! You okay?"

"I am fine damn it. Leave me alone!"

We were almost to the cabin. I sped up down the driveway, skidding to a stop before throwing the car into park.

"Max, are you feeling bad?" I turned to Max.

"Didn't I just say I am fine. You don't ever listen to me!"

"Baby! I think your sugar is high. Come in the house to get your shot. Can you walk?"

"Yes. You treat me like a baby," Max slurred out.

I jumped out, running around the car. I helped Max out of the car and into the house. I laid her on the couch while I ran to get her medicine. Max previously told me the dose she took. I got the shot ready. I unbutton Max's pants, pulled them down below her hip then rolled her to the side. "Stay still, Max!" I injected the shot into her hip causing Max to curse. Max hated the shot in her hip.

"You are okay, Max!" I rolled her onto her back. Between the ice cream and the adrenaline from the fight, her sugar was higher than we expected.

"I am tired," Max whispered.

"I know, baby. Let's go take a nap."

I helped Max to the bed then crawled in beside her. I turned to let Max spoon me. I felt an arm go around me and then it became heavy. Max fell asleep. I just laid there listening to Max breathe for about an hour before I found myself drifting off.

I woke up first and scooted out of bed. I grabbed the blood sugar kit and prepared it to take Max's sugar. I leaned over and whispered in Max's ear. "Hey, baby! I am going to make sure your blood sugar is good. You are going to feel a small stick."

Max held her finger out. Her eyes were still closed. I pricked her finger and tested the blood. It was 145. That was good. I slipped back in the bed. Max pulled me closer to her.

"What is it? Max asked.

"145," I answered.

Max nuzzled her face into my neck. "Sorry!"

"Hey, you can't help that, Max." I rolled over to face her. "Now it is your turn, Max. Tell me about your family."

Max slowly opened her eyes. "My dad and mom were great. I

am the only child. They were killed by a drunk driver when I was fourteen. I went to live with my aunt and uncle in Texas. They did the best they could to raise and provide for me. My life really wasn't rough just a difficult one. They gave me what I needed. They passed away years ago. I am by myself now other than just my friends."

I kissed her forehead. "You now have me. Thank you, Max, for today, last night, the whole weekend. No one has ever cared for me the way you have done. I don't know what I did to deserve your love."

I let my lips bite at Max's ear. Rolling my tongue over the lobe then moaning softly, I whispered, "Ask me what I want, Max."

Max breathed out, "What do you want, Sadie?"

I slipped my arm over Max's waist. "I want a fire!"

"Yes!" Max whispered inches from my lips.

I paused to lick Max's bottom lip. "I want wine."

"Yes, and what else, Sadie?" Max released a small moan.

I ran my fingers over Max's stomach. Max's body responded to my touch.

Our lips barely touched when I whispered out, "I want to kick your ass in a game of scrabble."

Max smiled keeping her lips inches from mine. "You are so wrong but a challenge accepted and the loser makes breakfast."

"Bring it!" I whispered.

The sand was falling!

16

"So, you once said you would follow me
anywhere,"
—Max

The bedroom was bright with sunshine radiating through the windows. Max rolled over in the bed. Her arm fell on the bed where I should be. She stretched and smiled as she pulled my pillow over her face. The smell of my hair lingered in the pillowcase as she inhaled deeply taking in the sweet scent. Rolling back over, she stretched again and took in the smell of the house. Someone lost the game last night, and the air was filled with the aroma of bacon and eggs.

"Good morning my sexy scrabble-losing baby!" Max said as she walked into the kitchen.

"Morning, baby. Did you sleep okay?" I asked as I shoved the bread in the toaster.

"I did."

Max walked up behind me kissing my neck softly before she poured herself a cup of coffee. "The best cup of coffee I had in a long time because you made it. I am starving." Max grabbed a piece of bacon before I swatted at her hand with a paper towel.

"Let's eat out on the patio. I already set the table." I turned around with a plate of bacon. "Oh, Max! Your eye is already turning black. Are you sure you are okay?" I reached toward the swollen eye.

"It hurts a little, but I will be fine." Max gave a wink with her good eye before grabbing another piece of bacon quickly.

Max helped me bring the food outside. "Did you call out sick today?

"Yes, I almost forgot." It was the last day of our trip, and it was gorgeous outside. We enjoyed breakfast taking in the fresh mountain air and beautiful skies.

"I thought we could take a hike today," Max said as she took the last bite of her eggs.

"That will be fun."

Max pulled me on her lap wrapping her arms around me tightly. "Be my girl, Sadie? I know we have things to work out but will you be mine? Only mine?" Max wrapped her fingers around my wrist.

"Yes, only yours!"

"I love you!" Max whispered.

"I love you more!" I softly whispered back.

We cleaned up and got dressed for the hike. Max grabbed a couple of waters before we headed to the trail that led us up to Mount Casejess. It was a small mountain, but the trail could be challenging at times with the tree roots and overgrown bushes. Max wrapped her fingers around my wrist and led me up the first part of the trail. We were close to midway when Max noticed I was breathing hard. She found a spot under a tree and helped me sit down.

"I am sorry, Max! I am really out of shape." I was trying to catch my breath.

"Let's stop here for a moment. We are almost to the top. Are you sure you are all right Sadie?" Max handed me a bottle of water. Max watched me as I gulped the water down. "Not too fast." Max pulled the water away from my lips.

"I feel better now. I think I am ready to keep going." I started to stand up.

Max suddenly pushed me back on the tree with her hand over my mouth. "Be quiet. There is a mother black bear with her cubs about a hundred feet away." Max pressed her body hard against mine. My chest was barely able to expand to catch a breath. I started to feel the panic overwhelming my body.

I shook my head to break my mouth free from the grasp. "Max, I can't handle you pushing me like this. He did this to me. You need to stop!" I started to squirm under Max.

"Baby, keep your voice down and look at me. I am not him. I am not going to hurt you but those bears will."

Max released the pressure a little, so I could take a deep breath. Max watched as the bears moved away slowly through the trees. They finally disappeared when Max relaxed taking in a deep breath.

"They are gone," Max said in a still whispered voice.

I laid my head back on the tree and took in deep breaths. "I'm okay. I'm okay. I'm okay," I kept repeating to myself.

Max pulled me into a soft embrace. "I am sorry, baby. I will never hurt you."

"I know. Let me shake it off." I buried my face into Max's neck. After a short while in Max's arms, I was relaxed again. I looked up at Max. "Seriously a bear?"

"Yes, a bear!"

"My life has been more exciting with you in the past few weeks than in my entire life. What else do you have exciting for me?"

"Oh, you have no idea, Sadie."

We laughed in each other's arms. Max held out her hand, and I slipped my wrist in the opened fingers. Max smiled before turning to head up the mountain. We were walking a little slower this time; the trees were thick barely letting the sunshine slip in. Pushing past a dense area of brush, the sky opened into a small cliff overlooking the most beautiful waterfall flowing into a small lake. The scenery was picture perfect, simply breathtaking.

"This is so amazing," I said as I admired the beautiful nature. I looked over the cliff staring into the clear blue water below. "Wow, look down there."

"So, you once said you would follow me anywhere," Max said with a smile.

"Yes," I said hesitantly.

Max looked over the cliff then back at me. "Ready to give it a go?"

"You got to be kidding. Right?"

I took a step back.

Max pulled me toward her. "You trust me?"

"You know I do."

"Take the leap with me, Sadie."

"We have clothes on, baby."

"That is an easy fix." Max kicked her shoes off, pulled her top off followed by her pants. Standing in nothing but her panties, she stepped toward me, reached out and pulled my top off. Max unbuttoned my jeans slipping them under my butt and pulling them all the way off. She leaned over and kissed my mound letting her mouth linger. Running my hand through her hair. This woman ignited my body on fire.

Max and I were standing together in nothing but panties. I looked over the cliff again.

"What the hell are we about to do?"

Max grabbed my wrist and pulled me to the edge of the cliff.

"Oh, my God!" I let it slip out of my mouth.

I felt my feet leave the ground, suddenly only air under me. Max was by my side on the way down and our hands connected as one. The fall seemed endless. The only sound filling the air was my screams echoing all around us. The splash was huge as we plunged into the water. The water was warm and soothing as it surrounded our bodies. We eventually stopped sinking and then we started swimming upward toward the sunlight, both taking in a gasp of air as we emerged breaking the surface of the water, our bodies coming up together holding each other tightly.

"You are crazy," I yelled out to Max.

Max laugh echoed around us. Then I joined in on the laugh because this was crazy as hell.

Max pulled me toward her. "Crazy about you!"

We swam over to the rocks edge by the waterfall. The rocks were wet and smooth to the touch. The pounding of the waterfall on the rocks deafened any other sounds around us.

Max backed me into the rocks. Her face buried into my neck kissing hungrily.

"I am so turned on!" Max whispered.

Max moaned as she cupped my breasts, lowering her mouth sucking hard on my wet nipples. Max pulled away looking at the hard nipple before she engulfed the nipple again. I shifted as I felt my vagina come to life. I placed my hand on Max's head then she sucked hard on my nipples. I moaned hard as I watched Max suck on me.

I arched backward moaning out. "Ah…that feels SOOO good!"

My moaning ignited Max's lust. Max moaned over the hardened nipples.

"Let me take you, Sadie" Max uttered with my hard nipple in her mouth.

"Yes, Max!"

Max pulled my panties down letting them float away. Max stood up turning me around, bending me over the rocks. Max spread my hands over the rocks.

"Keep your hands on the rocks. Do you understand, Sadie?"

"Yes, Max!"

Max placed her foot between my legs and opened them wide. She leaned over my body, her pussy laying on my ass. Max's hands ran over my thigh causing me to wiggle.

I felt the warm hands between my legs cupping my pussy. I laid on the rocks, which made my nipples aroused. I was grabbing the sides of the huge rock to brace myself. Max's lips kissed down the curve of my back. I felt Max's hand on my shoulder, then Max's lips kissing back up the curve of my back.

Max leaned over me whispering, "Tell me you want me inside you!"

"I want you in my pussy!"

Max stood up tightening her hold on my shoulder. Then her finger parted my pussy. Finding my hole, she let her finger slip deep inside my pussy. I arched in a long moan. "Ah…"

The sand was falling, and Max really knew how to make love.

Max leaned over my body with her own breast laying on my back, her finger slipping in and out slowly of my wet pussy before she started to pick up the pace. Max was getting aroused as she thrust harder.

She whispered in my ear between little moans that were escaping, "I am going to slip a second finger in."

Max wrapped her arm under me grasping at my breasts. Max's arm laid on the cool rock and my swollen nipples between her fingers. She twisted the nipple just as the second finger came to the edge of my pussy then dove deep joining the other wet finger.

"Ah… Max, don't stop."

"Fuck my finger, Sadie!" Max's fingers slipped all the way in filling me up, feeling so damned good.

My hips were starting to thrust; my grip tightened on the rocks. I was rocking back and forth, slow at first then the pace became faster. I was riding the hell out of Max's fingers long and hard.

Max's fingers felt way better than any dick I had ever had.

"Max…" I took small gasps of air. "Max, I am so close!"

"Let me feel you cum, Sadie!"

"Oh… fuck!" My pussy tightened into spasms as I released. My knuckles were white holding the edges of the rocks. Max rode my ass for a while as I climaxed feeling every muscle as they tighten in an explosion. My body was going limp on the rocks as the climax ended. I moaned when I felt Max's fingers slip out of me.

"Oh, my God, Max!" the last of my juices slipped out. I couldn't believe how Max made me cum.

Max was kissing my back softly. "You sounded so good. You have me wet, Sadie!"

I stood up twisting Max around letting her feel the cool rocks on her butt.

"Taking me like that turned you on, Max. You like fucking me?"

"Yes. I like fucking you."

"I like it too. I like you controlling me." I stepped in placing my body against Max. "Your nipples are so hard!" I whispered over

Max's lips as I twisted both nipples in my fingers.

"God, Sadie! You have me wanting to cum.…"

"Not yet baby. Pull your panties down and touch yourself."

Max was breathing hard. Her hand slipped down rubbing her pussy slowly. She released a moan as she felt her nipple become wet. Max looked down watching my mouth suck on the swollen nipple. Max watched as I moved down to her stomach. Her breathing increased as my tongue swirled around her belly button. Max's finger picked up speed. I kissed my way back up to Max's lips.

"My mouth has you turned on. Show me how low my mouth can go, baby," I said softly.

Max looked down. Taking her free hand, she drew an imaginary line across the top of her pussy. "Sadie, I…"

"I won't, baby" I took her finger and drew the same line across Max's belly. "I promise!"

I kneeled placing my hands on Max's hips. I sucked gently around the belly button before I let my tongue roll around then dip inside. Max moaned as she watched. Her own finger had slipped back inside her pussy. Her hips rose into my mouth as it slipped a little lower toward the invisible line she drew. My hands slipped behind her grabbing that tight ass. Max's free hand grabbed at my head as she felt soft licking above her pussy. Max had never been so aroused. It was causing her to want more. This was a feeling Max had never experienced, a feeling that was overwhelming all the fears that had dominated her life. Max wanted more for the first time in her life.

"Oh…Sadie, I am so wet. I want you to taste me, Sadie" Max gasped out.

I stopped long enough to pull away. "Baby, are you sure?"

"Yes, please!"

Max's eyes closed as she ushered my mouth down to her pussy. I was at the tip of her pussy feeling Max's finger below moving in and out slowly. Our eyes locked on each other for a moment before I lowered my face into Max's pussy. My tongue started licking softly up and down and all around, taking in the juices that were escaping. Licking and sucking made Max start to arch immediately, her ass rising off the rock.

"Sadie!" Max called out.

I knew my mouth on Max's pussy was a huge step toward healing. The last thing I wanted to do was to overwhelm her. I maneuvered up fast toward Max's mouth, our lips moaning over each other, my hand clawing at Max's breasts.

"Let go, baby" I moan out before I kissed Max passionately causing the start of a hard climax.

"OH… OH… OH shit!"

Max arched in a screaming moan, her climax exploding over and over again, my body riding the explosion, letting Max release all her juices. Her body collapsed. I wrapped Max up in a tight embrace as she started to shake uncontrollably.

"Sadie!" Max was barely able to speak.

"I am right here, baby" I whispered in Max's ear.

We laid there holding each other. Max finally stood up pulling her panties back up without saying a word. She became quiet and withdrawn.

"Max! What is going on? You okay?" I asked standing up in front of her. "Did I mess up when I placed my mouth on you?"

"No, Sadie! Not at all," Max answered back. "I wanted that physically so much, but now my brain has to process it. I am thinking too much right now, kind of mixed up in my head. I might not be able to do that again."

I stepped closer toward Max pulling her chin up, so our eyes met. "You wanted it physically because your brain knew it was right between two people who care for each other. If it happens again that is okay; if it doesn't that is okay too. You will know what you want, and I will be here for you. You can't shut down on me now,

Max. I need for you to talk to me about what's going on. Okay?"

"Okay, I didn't mean to shut down. I wanted … I REALLY enjoyed your mouth on me. Was it okay for me to want that, Sadie?"

"Baby, it was so normal. I feel so loved Max because you wanted me too." I kissed Max softly. "Thank you for loving me, Max."

"I love you so, Sadie. Thank you for being so caring, Sadie."

"We need each other. Remember, we promised we would fix each other. I wrapped my arms around Max's neck. "We do have one problem, Max."

"What is that, Sadie?" Max looked at me with a puzzled look.

"My panties are missing, and our clothes are twenty feet up there." I pointed upward while smiling in Max's eyes.

Max laughed. "That is fixable. Let's get climbing."

17

"Because we want to make sure you are
safe,"
—Lacey

It was two o'clock by the time Max and I gathered our clothes from the cliff and made it back to the cabin to pack and finally get on the road heading home. We decided to stop at the same diner on the way back to eat lunch.

The server, Sheila, was there with her same grease-stained uniform and crooked name tag. It was early Monday afternoon, so the diner had no customers.

"Have a seat anywhere, ladies," Sheila yelled out while she grabbed two menus.

Max noticed the cook staring at us as we walked over to the booth holding hands. Jerk! We sat at the same booth where we sat on Saturday. We ordered unsweet ice tea before looking at the menu.

Placing the two glasses of tea on the table, Sheila asked, "How was y'all's weekend?"

"It was amazing!" we said at the same time.

"We will have two club sandwiches with French fries," Max ordered for the both of us.

I looked across the table at Max smiling. She reached over and held my hand. "Max, can I ask a question?"

"Sure, Sadie. Is everything okay?

"Nothing is wrong. I have been trying to figure out something. Are you a dominant?"

Max paused for a moment before answering. "That is a complicated question," Max answered, thinking Sadie couldn't know of the lifestyle she lived before she met Zena.

"Try to explain it to me, Max. I am curious."

"How did you come to that conclusion, Sadie?"

"Little things but mostly the wrist holding is the biggest give away. You like to control things," I answered as I sipped my tea.

"I like to be the dominant one in a relationship, but that doesn't mean my girlfriend is submissive. It also doesn't mean I have whips, handcuffs and whatever else. Wait, I do have some of those things."

Max grinned.

I raised one eyebrow giving Max a look. Max smiled bigger.

"What is so funny?"

"Not funny but that raised eyebrow look is sexy. You just turned me on."

"You are impossible," I said in a smart tone.

"I have had relationships with submissive and non-submissive partners." Now, I feel like I'm rambling. "Yes, Sadie! I like to be dominant but please don't get scared of that. You don't have to be submissive to me."

"Relationships? So how many relationships have you had that you were submissive or non-submissive?" I asked curiously.

Max smiled. "I am not sure, but none compare to my love for you." She brought my hand up and kissed it softly.

"Smooth answer, Max. Was Zena a submissive?" I asked.

"Do you think Zena could ever be submissive? No, she wasn't." Max's tone changed. Max took a deep breath. "Okay, Sadie. You remember when we had sex in the beginning of our relationship? Remember how I controlled everything? I enjoyed that. I get off pleasing you. That was how all my relationships have been including Zena somewhat. I control how someone touches me or should I say how they don't touch me. With you..." Max paused. "With you it is different. I want to give all of me to you. I have never felt this way before with anyone. Hell! You were completely controlling me a few hours ago. I have never felt so aroused. I have never wanted anyone to put their mouth on my pussy like you did."

We were so deep in the conversation we didn't notice Sheila standing in front of us with a pitcher of tea.

"Um, need a refill?" Sheila asked as she stood there with a pitcher of tea.

"No!" we both chimed in at the same time never looking up at Sheila. Sheila turned around and walked away.

"So…do you want me to be submissive?" I asked.

"I want you to be mine. That is all. I want you to commit to me. Yes, I want to grab your wrist at times. Yes, I want to be able to control you in bed. But I will give you as much of me as I am able too." Max slipped her hands up and wrapped her fingers around my wrist. "Do you like when I do this?" Max asked.

"Yes!" I answered

"I am the only one who can do this now. You understand?"

"Yes," I answered very quietly. "Can I be the only one you do this too?"

"What do you mean?" Max asked.

"I saw you grab Zena's wrist the same way at the hospital," I said softly.

Max went quiet for a moment. "I am sorry, baby. That will not happen again. I didn't realize I did that. I was so mad that night."

"Okay," I answered in barely a whisper.

"Talk to me, Sadie. What is it?" Max asked. Shit! I have scared her.

I teared up. "My husband says he owns me and I am his. Did that make me his submissive?"

"No, Sadie. That made you the one that, that asshole abused." Max placed her hand on my heart. "This is what I want to be mine, Sadie. No one owns you, but your heart belongs to me if you want it to. A true dominant in a relationship would never abuse a sub. They get off pleasing them in all ways."

"Of course, I want my heart to belong to you. And Max…I think I may like being your sub."

"Your husband will be a thing of the past very soon. We will make sure of that. I love you, Sadie. If you turn out to be my submissive, that would be great, but if not, I am okay with that too."

"I love you too, Max!"

"Let's change the subject. When is your birthday, Sadie? You mentioned you were twenty-nine for a little while longer when we met."

"It is this Friday, the eighteenth."

"What would you like for your birthday?" Max asked.

"You have given me everything I could possibly want, Max." I just smiled.

"Well, Tori and Lacey want to know if we want to go out to dinner with them Friday, but if you don't want to, we can always say no to the invite."

"Dinner sounds great, Max. That will be nice to do together. Tell them yes."

Sheila brought over the plates and refilled the drinks. We enjoyed the sandwiches before we began the one-hour ride home.

We arrived in front of Max's apartment around five o'clock. Max jumped out and walked around helping me put my suitcase in my car. Standing on the sidewalk, Max pulled me in close, wrapping her arms around my waist.

"I have to work the next three days at the factory. I hate being away from you." Max laid her forehead on my forehead.

"I hate that you have to work twelve-hour shifts too."

"I will call you. Maybe you can come over after I get off," Max said as she pulled me closer.

"Of course, Max. You do know Zena is in your window watching us," I whispered in Max's ear.

"Then let's give her a show," Max said before her lips pressed softly against mine. Max's tongue slipped in slowly then out. Tasting so good.

I reached down and pulled Max's hand up placing it on my breast. "Make sure she gets her money worth!"

Max moaned as she squeezed softly. "Damn, now I want to take you to my bedroom and make love to you!" Max whispered over my lips.

"Get going. I have a feeling you have an apartment full of friends because Lacey's car is here also. I will talk to you later, baby. I love you and thank you for this weekend."

"Ugh, okay. I love you too." Max grabbed one more kiss before she pulled away and headed down the sidewalk.

I headed to my car. Jumping behind the wheel, I smiled while watching Max step into the breezeway of her apartment complex. I was happier than I have ever been in my life. I pulled out slowly from the parking space exiting to the street toward the left. A blue van made the left following close behind.

Max walked into her apartment to all her close friends sitting in the living room. She dropped her suitcase down before asking, "What's going on? Is this an intervention?" She smiled then headed to the kitchen opening the fridge grabbing a beer, twisting the cap off as she walked back in the living room. Max sat down in the recliner taking a swig of her beer.

"Holy shit! How did you get that shiner?" Tori asked.

"Oh, my God! Max, are you okay?" Colby asked.

Lacey walked over to take a close look at Max's face.

"Okay everyone, I am fine. I got in a fight this weekend. The other guy was left unconscious. So, I would say I got the better end of the fight," Max said as she shooed Lacey away.

"How was your weekend Max other than kicking a little ass?" Tori asked.

"Yeah, I am sure you got a lot of ass also," Zena mumbled from the corner of the room.

Max turned her beer up while she shot Zena a glare. "It was great. Colby, what is going on?" It was obvious Colby was on edge about something. Max had always been able to tell what type of mood Colby was in.

"Lacey has something to tell you," Colby said looking away.

"Spill it, Lacey," Max started to sound agitated.

"We all love you, Max. While you were gone, we figured we would check out Sadie." Lacey started to say before Max stopped her.

"WE? Who is we? Colby and Tori, are the two of you part of this shit" Max's voice was raised.

"It wasn't our idea, but we also didn't stop it," Colby answered,

"It is all of us, Max. Just listen before you blow." Tori chimed in.

"I ran her license plate and found out the car is not in her name. It belongs to a Reeva Walsh in upstate New York. I ran a check on Sadie Jones and nothing came back matching Sadie's description."

"Why would you do that?" Max balled her fist up.

"Because we want to make sure you are safe," Lacey answered.

"The fucking person who made me spiral out of control is in this room, but you feel the need to check out the one person who really cares about me." Max' voice was filled with irritation.

Zena stayed in the corner until she heard Max's words then she lurched toward Max. "Is that what she did all weekend, fucking take care of you, Max? Did she fuck you? Because I sure as hell couldn't."

Max bolted out of the recliner knocking over her beer. "No, you couldn't fuck me but you sure as hell could fuck that slut from the city. I am so sick of your bullshit."

"You want to know what I am sick of, Max? The Maxine pity train is what I am sick of. Poor me! I got cheated on so let me try to kill myself."

"Why are you such a bitch?"

Max and Zena were toe to toe before Tori jumped between them.

"Damn it! Zena, step back, and Max sit down!" Tori ordered.

Zena turned and walked away mumbling back to the corner.

Max walked to the backside of the recliner leaning over it. She was rocking in anger.

"Everyone here needs to back off," Max said as she lowered her head. "Let me handle this. If I need to talk to you, I will, but all of you need to trust me."

"We like Sadie. We really do, Max. We just love you, and we are so scared that you will get hurt again. Something was going on with her, Max, and we are scared that it will hurt you also." Colby spoke out. He walked over and was rubbing Max's back.

"Colby, please don't touch me right now. I know what is going on and she and I are dealing with it. She will not hurt me like some people. I have been able to talk to her and open up. I am falling in love with her."

"I can't deal with this bullshit." Zena grabbed her purse and stormed out of the apartment, slamming the door behind her.

Tori looked over at Lacey. "Go check on her."

Lacey walked out quickly to catch up with Zena.

"Max, we just care," Tori said.

"I know Tori, but you did not have the right to investigate her like a criminal. I need some air." Max grabbed her keys and opened the door.

"Max?" Colby stepped closer. "Please don't go!"

Max walked out of the apartment feeling frustrated and full of anger, slamming the door behind her. As far as she was concerned, her friends had crossed a line. Before Max knew it, she was peeling out of the parking lot. She sped past Zena and Lacey standing by Zena's car. She never looked over at them. All she knew was she needed to get away.

I pulled in front of Mrs. Preakness house; it started to rain. Running inside quickly before the bottom dropped out of the sky, I threw the suitcase on my bed and opened it. I had a lot of laundry to do before I returned to work the next day. Pulling my clothes out of the suitcase the disposable phone fell on the floor. I leaned over picking the phone up before sitting down on the bed. My fingers ran over it then I turned it on. I sat there staring at the phone for the longest time. My fingers started to dial my sister's phone number.

"Hello!"

"Hello!"

"Hey, sis!" I finally said.

"You okay?" Patsy asked.

"I am fine. Just wanted to hear your voice again." My voice was trembling as we spoke. "I am going to be there in a month. I must end my marriage. I met someone."

"You have? Tell me!" Patsy asked.

"Not right now, Patsy. Is the money I took before I left in a safe place?"

"Yes, the 300,000 dollars is hidden with no paper trail to follow. Do you need money?" Patsy asked. "I can get you some."

"No, Patsy. I can't take the chance. I am okay. I have to go, but I will see you next month for the divorce hearing. Love you, sis!"

"Love you too!"

The blue van continued down the road past the house. The woman in the van saw the figure of someone running inside trying to dodge the drops of rain. The van rounded the corner and pulled into a gas station coming to a stop. The woman driving picked up a phone and dialed a number. She sat there patiently waiting for the man to pick up the other end.

"Yes," the man answered.

"I lost her for three days, but she finally showed back up" the woman blew a puff of smoke out of the van window.

"Call me if there are any changes. I will be arriving Friday." The man slammed the phone down.

18

"We went too far, Tori,"
—Colby

Rain was pounding against the window sill relentlessly. I rolled over to my side of the bed watching the stream of water slipping down the wall from a crack in the window. My previous life felt like that crack slowly leaking into the new life. How am I going to be able to fix the leak? I rolled to my back looking at the cracks in the ceiling. "Fuck! These damn cracks need to get out of my life!" I closed my eyes imagining a life with Max. I whispered softly, "I have to seal the cracks." I looked over at the clock. It was almost nine. I flipped the hourglass over before I picked up my phone to text Max.

Tks 4 an unforgettable weekend. So glad we took the leap together. Nite, Sexy.

Text sent.

Colby and Tori were still waiting for Max to return. Max had been gone for hours. Lacey headed off with Zena to get a few drinks.

"We went too far, Tori," Colby said.

"I am thinking the same thing, Colby. We will make it right. Max knows we care."

"I know we care, Tori, but we have to let Max try life herself. We can't keep trying to control her life. We need to just be there if she gets hurt."

"You are right, Colby," Tori said as she looked at the clock. "Where the hell is Max?"

"Did you hear something, Tori?" Colby asked as he sat on the edge of the couch. "There it is again. It is coming from the recliner."

Tori reached down the side of the chair pulling out Max's phone. "She must have dropped it when she jumped up at Zena. The text was from Sadie. Max isn't with her. I am going to text her back."

Hey Sadie, this is Tori. Max got mad at us and stormed out hours ago. She dropped her phone. We can't find her. Have you seen her?

Text sent.

No. She isn't with me. What happened?

Text received.

We will tell you later. I am worried about her. Let us know if you see her. Please!

Text sent.

Let me know if she comes home.

Text received.

I jumped out of bed quickly throwing on a pair of sweatpants and sweatshirt. There was no way I was going to lay around waiting for a text. I needed to find Max.

Opening the front door of the house a crack of lightning struck causing me to jump back. I looked out into the fogged-up glass of the front door. I pulled the raincoat hood over my head before I stepped out onto the leaking porch. Every nook and cranny leaked in this house. I unlocked the car before I stepped out in the pouring rain. I stopped suddenly when the front of the car caught my eye. I squinted trying to see through the rain. Was that Max's car? The car was parked on the side of the house.

"What the hell!" I mumbled.

I ran across the wet ground jumping a few puddles and landing in a few. I looked through the driver's window. It was empty. I stepped into a puddle so I could look through the back window. Max was curled in a ball with a blanket covering her body. I opened the door and jumped in quickly before slamming the door behind me. The first thing I noticed was the six-pack of beer with four empty bottles on the floorboard.

"Hey, Max! What is going on, baby?" I asked as I removed the wet raincoat.

"They pissed me off, Sadie!" Max answered as she tilted the

fifth beer up.

"Give me this so I can crawl in next to you," I said as I took the beer away from Max placing it back inside the six-pack container. I slipped under the blanket with Max.

"That rain is freezing." Wrapping my arms around Max's waist, I kissed Max softly on the forehead. "What happened?" I just had to ask.

"They have no right…." Max said with a slur. "My friends tried to investigate you."

"Why would they do that, Max?"

"Ohhhh! Because they say they are SOOO worried about me. And you're hurting ME!" Max started raising her voice.

I pulled Max closer to me. "What did they find out?"

"Nothing but your car isn't your car. They suck as private eyes!" Max laid her head back. "The room is swirling."

"You are in your car, baby. Put your foot on the floorboard for me. That will help." I helped Max move her foot to the floor of the car. "I wish they hadn't done that, but I doubt they found out anything. It is okay, Max. Don't let this get to you."

"My life, Sadie! They need to let me live it. Damn that foot thing works," Max said as she looked around. "I am going to call you, but I can't find my phone."

Max's words were mixing up. She was drunk.

"Tori has your phone back at the apartment," I answered.

"Max, I need to text them and tell them I found you. They are worried about you," I said softly in Max's ear before I kissed her.

"Whatever. I could care less about them. Stop whispering in my ear. You are turning me on!" Max mumbled out.

"Everything turns you on, Max!" I giggled.

"Your breast turns me on." Max went under my shirt cupping at my breast. Max was kissing on my neck when I started the text to Tori.

I found Max. She was in front of my place. I live at Mrs.

Preakness' house on Fourth Avenue, the house where you and Max installed the water heater. Bring me the testing kit so I can check her sugar.

Text sent.

We were on our way!

Text received.

While I was trying to text, Max pulled my shirt up. I did not have on a bra because I left in such a rush. Max's mouth was sucking on my right nipple. Max bit down hard on the swollen nipple.

"Ouch! Okay, baby! We are not having sex right now." I pulled Max's mouth away from my breast then quickly pulled down the sweatshirt. "I think someone is drunk."

"I am buzzed. Not drunk, Sadie," Max replied.

"Sit up for me," I ordered as I pulled on Max. "Hey, there sexy!" I said as I helped Max catch her balance.

"This weather sucks," Max wrote M.S. loves S.J on the fogged-up window.

"Such a romantic!" I said as I drew a heart around the initials.

A tall vehicle pulled in front of Max's car; the headlights blinded us. We covered our eyes until the lights went off. After a few seconds, Tori and Colby jumped in the front seats of the car. They both looked like a couple of drown rats.

"Why are you here? I don't want to talk," Max said locking eyes with the two of them.

"We need to talk," Tori answered.

"Give me the kit," I said. Colby passed the kit to me.

"Max, let me check your sugar levels."

Max sat there holding out her finger while staring at the two wet rats in the front seat. I stuck Max with the needle drawing blood for the test. I looked at the results. "It is high but not too bad. It is 212. You will need insulin soon, Max."

Colby looked at me before asking politely. "Will you come to

Tori's truck, Sadie? Let Tori and Max talk."

Max looked over at Sadie before telling her. "Go ahead." Max watched Sadie run in the rain and try to heave herself up into Tori's truck.

"Damn, she has a sexy ass," Max said aloud.

Tori twisted her body around to face Max in the back seat. "I am so sorry, Max. We are totally out of line. It won't ever happen again."

"You damn straight it won't! All of YOU were out of line," Max mouthed back. "Everyone needs to back the fuck off! I would have expected that out of Zena and even Lacey but not you and Colby. That really hurt the most."

"We thought we were protecting you, but all we did was made you upset. You are my family, Max. I love you like my own blood. Please forgive me! Please forgive all of us!"

"I swear if this happens again!" Max was tearing up.

"It won't, Max. I promise. You know we are here if you need us."

"I know that, Tori, but I have to try this relationship. I am in love with this woman. She was nothing like Zena. She would not hurt me in the way Zena did."

"We all will back off. I promise. We good, Max?"

"You know I can't stand being mad at you, Tori. We are good. But I am not good with Zena. I am so sick of her crap, Tori. I don't want her around anymore. Her snide remarks need to end."

"I know, Max. I just don't know how to fix that."

"Just keep her crazy ass away from me and Sadie!"

"You are buzzing hard, Max," Tori said.

"Yeah, I am pretty fucked up." Max laughed. "But I mean what the hell I said."

Colby and I were watching Max and Tori talking. The rain

started to ease up.

"Sadie, we screwed up!" Colby finally said.

"Max told me what happened and I know that everyone meant well, but there has to be a limit, Colby. I am in love with Max. It would break my heart if I ever hurt any part of her."

"She loves you too, Sadie" Colby answered. "Tori and I talked, and we are just hurting Max. We must let Max figure things out for herself. It won't happen again."

I asked Colby, "Can you get everyone together tomorrow night at your place?

"I am sure I can but why Sadie?"

"If you can just do it, please. Maybe around 5:30 pm or 6:00 pm would be great," I said before I jumped out of the truck and headed back to Max's car.

I jumped in the driver's seat.

"Tori, can you call Max out of work tomorrow, please? You ready to go home, Max?"

"Yes," Max answered as she opened the door and stood outside in the rain.

Tori reached over and hugged me.

"It is okay, Tori!"

"HELLO! I am getting wet out here!" Max yelled at the sky with her head back.

Tori jumped out of the car hugging Max for the longest time. The rain didn't exist to them at that moment.

Colby ran over and hugged Max before jumping in the backseat behind me. Max was drenched by the time she got in the car. I took both home. The thunder was pounding, and the lightning was cracking in the sky. The rain had finally stopped. Colby and I helped Max out of the car and headed toward the apartment when Max suddenly stopped and looked at me.

"She is going to puke, Colby!" I yelled out just as Max leaned over and let go of her stomach into a bush. I held her hair back as she heaved at least four times before Colby and I were finally able to get Max in the apartment.

"Go take a hot shower, Max, while I fix you a sandwich." I pushed the bathroom door open guiding Max toward the shower.

Max got in the shower and let the hot water hit all over her body.

After a few, Max got out of the shower and sat down on the bed. I joined her with a plate and her insulin shot. "Eat this; then I will give you your insulin. You need to get in bed and sleep off this buzz as you called it." I handed Max a plate then leaned over and kissed her softly.

"I am not hungry!" Max grumbled placing the plate on the bed.

"Then let me give you your shot." I pulled the towel away from Max's thigh.

"No!" Max hit at my hand.

"Max, we are not doing this tonight. Sit still for me."

Max sat completely still and pouting as I injected the needle. I leaned over and kissed Max's thigh then laid my head on Max's lap.

Max rubbed my head. "Sorry, baby! Didn't mean to get grumpy!"

"I know, sweetheart. Let's lay in the bed after you eat this sandwich for me please." I sat up handing Max the plate.

Max ate the sandwich before we crawled into bed. I pulled the covers up and over us making us cozy in the bed together. I rolled over in our position so Max could spoon me. I felt Max's face nuzzle into the back of my neck then Max's arm fell across my waist.

"Night, baby!" Max mumbled.

"Night!"

19

"The truth will come out soon enough,"
—Lacey

Max walked from the bedroom into the kitchen. She sat down on the bar stool placing her head down on the counter. Colby just finished making a pot of coffee, and the toaster popped up revealing two English muffins. Colby poured a cup of coffee for Max and handed it to her.

"You want something to eat?" Colby asked.

"No, Did Sadie go to work?"

"She left around 8:30. You okay?" Colby asked as he sat beside Max.

"Yeah! Drinking is a stupid choice to make," Max rubbed her temples.

"Yes, it is my dear friend, but the reason you got drunk is even more stupid." Colby laid his head on her shoulder. "I am sorry again, Max. I tossed and turned all night thinking of what we had done."

Max wrapped her arms around Colby. "We will get past it, Colby. I know I put all of you through so much. I know I scared you. I am sorry, but I am better, Colby. I am in love again."

Colby kissed Max's shoulder and gave her a tight hug.

"Max, Sadie asked me to get us all together tonight for a meeting here at 5:30."

"Why?" Max asked.

"She didn't say."

"Hmm, don't ask Zena." Max sipped her coffee. "Colby, I need to ask you something."

"Sure, Max."

Max turned toward Colby, "I want to ask Sadie to move in here with us. The place she lives in is a dump."

Colby was quiet for a moment. "The extra money toward the rent will be nice. Having her here will make you happy, so the answer is yes, Max. Of course, she can move in." Colby wrapped his arms around Max in another tight hug.

Max walked around into the kitchen and topped off her cup of coffee. "I am going to go take a shower and go shopping for Sadie's birthday. We were going to have dinner for her birthday on Friday, and then I figured we would come by your bar for some dancing. Colby, you want to come with me shopping?"

"Girl!" Colby started snapping his fingers. "You know I am not turning down any shopping trips." Colby clapped his hands together. "Let's go to the sex store!"

Max laughed out.

It was close to 4:30 p.m. when Max and Colby arrived back at the apartment from shopping. Max pulled into the parking space, and she noticed Sadie leaning on her car talking to a woman who lived a couple complexes down from Max's apartment. The woman had one arm on the car and was leaning into Sadie. She was way too close to Sadie.

Colby looked over at Max starring at them. "They are just talking, Max. Don't lose it!"

Max got out of the car and approached the two of them. Sadie didn't notice Max coming up from behind her until she felt Max's hand grab her wrist then felt the pull causing Sadie to slide off the car. Max pulled Sadie behind her with a tight grip. Max just stood there looking at the woman until the woman turned around and walked off. She yelled back at Max, "You better collar her, Max." Max didn't say a word as she pulled Sadie behind her toward the apartment. I was double stepping trying to keep up.

"Baby, what the hell?" "Slow down!" You were going to pull my arm out of the socket," I shouted while stumbling behind Max.

Colby's hands were full of packages as he walked behind them.

Once in the apartment, Max dragged me straight to the bedroom. She slammed the door behind us. She pulled me into a big tight hug. She kissed me passionately pushing me against the wall.

"Don't push me too hard against the wall!" I gasped out.

Max pulled away then whispered softly, "I'm sorry, baby!"

Max kneeled and removed my panties from under my skirt then she hiked the skirt above my thighs. She opened my legs and put her mouth around my pussy, diving her tongue in and out of my pussy, licking, sucking and kissing all over.

"Oh geez!" My head tossed back against the wall while I laid my hand on Max's head. Max's head was bobbing back and forth as she ate my pussy.

The tip of her tongue rolled between my clit then circled my pussy before she sucked harder. Max's wet fingers easily slipped inside my so wet pussy. Max could hear me moaning harder as her fingers filled me. Max grabbed my ass pulling me into her face with her eager mouth open and tongue diving in and out of my pussy. The wet finger slipped out. Max spread my lips wide with her fingers before her tongue dipped inside of me again and again until...

"OH. OH! Max!" I screamed out.

Max slipped her finger back into me while she pulled her tongue out of my pussy. Max was slowly letting the fingers slip in then out, watching the fingers disappear inside then coming out covered in juices. The sound of light slapping as the finger started to move faster could be heard. My walls were starting to tighten around her fingers.

"Max! ... Max! ..." I pushed Max's mouth into my pussy as I exploded everywhere.

Max filled me up with her tongue and fingers, then sucking, made all the juices slide out. I exploded twice before I pulled Max's mouth away. It was feeling so damned good. I didn't want her to stop, but I just couldn't take anymore.

"Jesus, Max!" Oh, my! No one has ever made me feel this good and make me cum so many times before.

Max kissed me from my pussy to my mouth. She whispered

over my lips "You taste so damned good. Put your arms above your head." I raised my arms slowly. Max unbuttoned her pants and yanked them along with her panties down below her ass. Max held my arm against the wall. Burying her face into my neck, Max touched herself. Max moaned into my neck a few times before she exploded.

Max pulled away and backed up to the bed pulling her pants up as she sat down. I joined her and sat there.

"You okay, Max?"

"Yes!"

"What was that all about?"

"I don't like that woman you were talking to. She tried to screw one of my old girlfriends. I know her from this club I belong too. She was about to kiss you. I was jealous."

"Baby! You have no reason to be jealous."

"You are so naïve, Sadie."

"I am not that naïve, Max. I know no other lips will ever touch me but yours."

Max smiled. "Your green-eyed monster loves you. You mad at me?"

"No, but that part of you threw me off a little. Not that I am complaining about the sex because it is great, but sometimes we can talk through things too. I am not going to cheat on you, Max. I promise. So get that out of your mind." I rubbed Max's back softly.

"I am sorry." Max covered her face with her hands.

"It is okay, Max." I pulled Max's hands away. "It is kind of cool having someone who loves me enough that they are jealous. Now, what club?"

"A club in the city. Don't worry. I haven't been there in over three years. You like me being jealous over you, huh?" Max pulled me on her lap.

"Yes, it is very sexy. Max, I told Colby to tell your friends to come over. I am going to talk to them, but I will tell them what I think they need to know. Maybe it will help, maybe not. Come on. Let's go wait for them."

I jumped off Max's lap.

"I will be there in a moment," Max said.

"Don't be long okay," I said as I put my panties back on and walked out.

Max walked over to the dresser and looked at herself in the mirror. She popped open the bottle of pills and swallowed two of them. She placed the cap back on and threw the bottle at the mirror before she buried her face in her hands.

"You okay, Sadie? You are flushed." Colby made the observation as I walked into the living room. Just then there was a knock at the door. Colby jumped up to answer it.

"Hey, guys!" Colby said as he let Tori and Lacey in.

They both greeted Sadie and sat down on the couch. Max walked out of the bedroom. Lacey stood up giving her a hug then whispering something in her ear.

Max shook her head in a yes motion. Max sat down on the arm of the chair where I was sitting.

I asked, "Is Zena coming?"

"No!" Lacey answered followed by no explanation.

I laid my hand on Max's leg. "Max told me what caused the fight between all of you. So, I want to explain a few things. You are right there is something in my past. Max knows about it. I have told her everything. I am going through a divorce that isn't pretty. That is why the car is not in my name. Reeva is the cousin of an old friend of mine who let me use her car to get away."

"Why do you have to get away, Sadie? Lacey asked.

"You don't need to know everything, Lacey," Max blurted out.

I wrapped my fingers around Max's upper arm to calm her down. "It is okay, Max.

"He is ugly and vindictive, so I decided I will stay out of his way until we go to court next month."

"Is he violent?" Tori asked.

"He can be Tori, but only toward me," I answered.

"He caused the scar?" Colby asked.

"What scar?" Lacey chimed in.

I pulled up my shirt to reveal the scar. "This is the scar Colby is talking about. I know Tori and Colby have seen it. And no, he didn't cause it. It happened when I was young, and I tried to jump a barb wired fence."

Max reached over and pulled my shirt down. "That is enough."

"Max, I want them to understand that I care for you and I am not going to hurt you," I said as I rubbed Max's arm.

"What if he shows up here?" Tori asked.

"My family is in upstate New York, and they have been keeping an eye on him. He doesn't know where I am. While we were away at the cabin… I looked over at Max. "We both opened up about our past. I care about this woman, and I would never hurt her. I know all of you are protective of Max and I know why. But you don't have to protect her from me." Looking over, Max had tears in her eyes. I wiped a tear away.

"I am sorry, Sadie, about trying to find out more about you," Lacey said. "But why couldn't I find a match for you. No social media account could be found. Who doesn't have a social media account nowadays? I couldn't find anything on you."

"Kind of hard to have a social media account when you are trying to get away from someone. I had a pretty boring life before I arrived in Pulse. So, I am sure you won't find me on the Internet either," I replied.

"I need a beer," Max chimed out as she stood up.

"Oh. No, you don't!" I pulled Max down on the arm of the chair.

"Do you have any more questions?" Max asked the group.

"We are good, Max and Sadie," Tori said.

"But…" Lacey chimed in before being cut off by Tori.

Tori glared at Lacey, "We are good, Lacey."

Suddenly, there was a knock at the door. Lacey stood up to go answer it.

"That better not be Zena!" Max said.

"It is Chinese food. I ordered Chinese for everyone," Lacey said as she opened the door to reveal a delivery man with his arms filled with bags.

Everyone enjoyed the Chinese food for the next hour. The atmosphere in the room changed to a light conversation. Tori and Lacey told everyone they picked a date for the wedding, which would be next year. Colby told us he met a new guy over the weekend. No one talked about Zena, not even Lacey. Max reached over and opened a fortune cookie. She read it to herself and placed it in her pocket.

"What did it say?" I asked.

"My future is right in front of me!" Max smiled.

I stretched up and kissed Max softly. "Yes, it is!" I whispered.

"I have to get to work," Colby said. "Tonight is Tickle Tuesday at MadJax."

"That sounds gross, Colby," Max said.

"Depends on who is doing the tickling." Colby jumped up landing on Max, his hands tickling her sides. Max started to laugh before she pushed him away. "See, depends on who is tickling you."

"Such a dumb queen but I love my dumb queen," Max said as she shook her head.

"Lacey and I need to get going too. We will walk out with you, Colby."

"We still good for Friday night?" Max asked.

"Of course, where are we eating?" Tori asked.

"Sadie's call. It is her birthday!" Max looked over at me.

"Larry's" I answered.

"Larry's it is. 6:00 okay?" Max said as she walked everyone to the door.

"Perfect!" Lacey kissed Max on the cheek before leaving.

Tori and Lacey got in the truck. Lacey was staring at the window looking into Max's apartment.

"Lacey, leave it alone," Tori said.

"She didn't tell us everything. I know there is more."

"Drop it, Lacey. We are not going to fight over this!"

Tori started the truck. "The truth will come out soon enough," Lacey said as she lit a cigarette.

Max and I cleaned up the leftovers. Lacey had ordered enough for twenty people. The clock was showing 8:00 pm. Max grabbed my wrist and started to walk me to the bedroom.

"Hey, I really should go home. I have no clothes for work tomorrow," I said as I stopped walking behind Max.

Max turned around and stepped toward me pulling me closer. "Stay tonight and sleep with me. I have to be at work at 7:30. If you get up with me, you will have time to go grab some clothes. I want to fall asleep with you in my arms and hold you tonight." Max made a pouty face.

"Okay baby! I want your arms and body around me too."

20

"I think you wore me out,"
—Max

It was FRIDAY finally, and it was Sadie's birthday. Max was in the kitchen making me a birthday breakfast. I was still in bed sound asleep. There was a knock at the door, Max turned off the burner on the stove then headed toward the door. She peeked through the peephole in the door. A tall man was standing on the other side of the door. He was well built with light brown hair and had five o'clock shadow on his face. He was a well-dressed man wearing a gray suit. Max opened the door slowly.

"Good morning, ma'am. Are you Maxine Shields?" he asked.

"Yes, can I help you?" Max answered.

"I am Mr. Smith with Old Insurance Co. I am here to appraise the damage done to your vehicle by our client. Can you step outside to look at the car?"

"Sure. Hold on a minute." Max grabbed her keys, closing the door quietly so she would not wake me.

Walking to the car, the man walked behind Max. They looked at the damage, and the man made notes and took pictures.

"Was that damage already there prior to the accident?" The man pointed to the bumper of the car."

"I don't see what you are talking about," Max replied.

"Let me help you see it." The man wrapped his hand around the back of Max's neck. His fingers tightened down as he pushed her toward the car. Max pulled out of his grip giving the man a glance as she rubbed the back of her neck.

"Sorry! I don't know my own strength sometimes," he responded to Max's glare. "Just one more question. The lady that was with you, was she hurt?"

"No, she wasn't," Max responded.

"How is Miss Jones related to you?" the man asked as he looked through papers.

"She is my girlfriend. How do you know her name?"

"It's in the report. What do you mean girlfriend? Like a friend that is a girl or a girlfriend who you are fucking? Do you fuck her with your make-believe dick?" The man voice trailed off so low Max couldn't hear him.

"Sorry! What did you just say?" Max asked in a harsh tone.

"Nothing, I got what I need." The man walked away getting into a huge 4x4 truck.

"What a jerk!" Max said as she walked back into the apartment.

The man pulled the truck over and made a phone call to woman in the blue van. "I am here!" He hung up quickly. He ran his hands through his hair before balling up his fists. His face tensed up causing the veins in his forehead to pop out. He began to pound his fist into the rear-view mirror. The frame broke first followed by the entire mirror breaking off the windshield. "BITCH! That fucking BITCH!" he screamed as he watched blood pour over his knuckles.

I rolled over, stretching in the bed. The sun was up, and I looked over at the clock. It was almost 10:30 am. I jumped up quickly. I refocused my eyes to make sure it was really 10:30 am.

"Shit!" I mumbled out.

"What is the matter?" Max said as she came into the bedroom with a tray of pancakes and bacon.

"I am late for work!"

"I called your boss and told him that you would not be in today," Max said as she laid the tray across my lap.

"What? What did you tell him?"

"I told him it is your birthday and you will not be in today because you are going to be fucked really good by your girlfriend." Max giggled as she grabbed a piece of bacon.

"No, you didn't!"

"Okay I didn't, if you say so!" Max shrugged her shoulders. "I guess you will find out on Monday."

I smiled. "You are impossible. What is all of this?"

"Just a little nourishment for the birthday girl. You will need your strength." Max held the bacon in front of my mouth. "Take a bite!"

I finished every bite of my birthday breakfast. Max pulled the tray away and sat it on the floor. I rolled over to the opposite side of the bed and jumped out.

"Where are you going?" Max asked.

"First to the bathroom but I really need to go home and wash a load of laundry. I have been here every night this week. I will be right back!"

I grabbed my toothbrush off the dresser. I returned a few minutes later to Max sitting on the side of the bed. I walked over, stood between Max's legs and pulled Max's hair back into a ponytail.

"Shit! I left my toothbrush in the bathroom," I said as I took a step back.

"Leave it there, Sadie!" Max pulled me back in between her legs.

"I will need it later."

Max pulled out a small box with a red bow around it. "Leave it there!" Max said as she handed the box to me.

I took the box and examined it by turning it over then shaking it side to side. "You didn't have to get me anything."

"Just open it!" Max said.

I pulled on the bow and lifted the lid off. I looked into the box. Lying on a bed of cotton was a single key.

"Move in with me, Sadie," Max said.

The sand was falling.

I picked the key up. "Yes," I mouthed the words, but no sound came out.

"Was that a yes?" Max could not hear any words come out of my mouth.

"That's a YES!" I said in a much louder voice.

Max pulled me down on top of her kissing me on the way to the bed. Max ran her hands under my shirt scratching my back. I moaned into Max's mouth. Max rolled over pulling me under her.

"I have another present for you," Max said as she reached under the pillow. "Happy birthday, Sadie!"

The box was bigger than the other one but with the same red bow. I pulled the bow off first then opened the box. I looked inside suddenly cocking my head sideways.

"It is a toy for you!" Max said.

"Okay, but I don't know what to do with—this…" I said as I pulled the dildo out along with an array of straps.

"Well! First, you have to name her."

"Name her? You want me to name a dildo?"

"Yes! Give her a name, Sadie." Max smiled as she took the straps from me.

"Okay, I guess I will name her Delta," I said amused.

"Delta? Okay, Delta it is." Max leaned over and whispered in my ear. "Delta and I want to fuck the birthday girl. Tell me what the birthday girl wants."

I thought for a moment. "Stand up and put the straps on."

Max hurried up and stripped in front of me. Then she wrapped the straps around her waist, then between her legs, hooking all the buckles. Max took Delta from me and attached her to the harness. Looking Max up and down, I peeled my top off followed by my pajama bottoms.

"I think I want to be a dominant, Max!" I said as I kicked my panties across the room.

"Okay, Sadie, for your birthday, but you know the boundaries."

"I know, Max. Will Delta please you at all?

"If she rubs against me in the right way."

"Kneel, Max, between my legs. Slip your fingers into me!"

"Yes, ma'am."

Max spread my legs and slipped a finger inside of me. I moaned as my arms wrapped around Max's neck. I watched as Max's fingers entered my pussy then pulled out. "OH! Max, suck my nipple." Max began sucking slowly then pulling the nipple with her teeth before sucking harder.

"Don't make me cum, Max," I said through heavy breaths.

I slipped Max's finger out slowly. I scooted onto the bed pulling Max on top of me. I reached down grabbing Delta guiding the head to my pussy opening. Max grabbed the base of Delta waiting to enter Delta into me.

I pulled Max's ear to my mouth then whispered. "Fuck me but don't you cum until I do!"

"Yes, ma'am! Don't let me hurt you!"

Max pushed the head into me. I arched in pleasure. "Oh fuck!" Max pushed Delta farther in until she felt our pussy's touch.

"You okay?" Max whispered in my ear.

"Oh, yes," I moaned back in Max's ear.

Delta filled my pussy. Max straightened her arms pulling herself over the top of me. She started to rub slowly in circles, leaning over sucking gently on my hard nipples. I moaned one after another as I grasped at the sheets. I am starting to thrust upward into Max causing Delta to go deeper. Delta was hitting all the right spots.

"Harder Max!" I gasped out as I pulled Max down on me. My fingernails dug into Max's back.

Max moaned deeper as she began to thrust in and out faster and harder, her ass rising then diving deep in causing our pussies to slap together.

"Sadie!" Max groaned out.

"A little longer, Max!" I moaned out as I wrapped my legs around Max.

"Fuck!" Max thrust deep and rubbed up and down before pulling Delta back to the edge of the hole.

I threw both arms above her head. "Max, grab my wrist" I was breathing hard. Max reached up holding my hands down by the wrists above my head. "God, Sadie" Max's ass was thrusting and rubbing fast and hard. My legs were interlocked around Max. The bed was rocking back and forth making this loud noise as it pounded the wall. Max was fucking me really hard with Delta. This felt so good. I had never had anyone to screw me like this.

"Right there, Max. Oh yes! Don't stop! Oh! I need you to cum, Max." I arched hard screaming in ecstasy twisting my body into Max as I exploded over Delta. Delta made my juices squirt out of me several times. My body squirted juices like it had never done before.

Max arched at the same time exploding hard. "Ah! I am cumming, Sadie!"

Our explosions lasted forever until we both collapsed with Delta between them. Delta was covered in mixed juices. Max and I could barely breathe. Max slowly reached down, grabbing Delta by the base then she slipped her out of me. I moaned as the head fell free out of me.

"Happy birthday, Sadie from me and Delta!" Max said as she rolled over.

I rolled over to face Max. "I love you and Delta."

Max smiled into my eyes, "I love you too!"

We tossed Delta to the side onto the floor then Max pulled the blanket over our naked, tired bodies. We laid there in silence listening to each other breathe. Before we realized it, we drifted off to sleep. The sex drained us, but it was fantastic, so I did not mind.

There was knocking on the door. Max opened her eyes to see if I was still asleep.

"You two up? We have to leave in an hour," Colby screamed through the door.

"Yeah, we are up!" Max screamed back.

"Wake up, Sadie! We need to get ready to leave."

"I blinked my eyes trying to open them and to focus on the

clock. I rolled over swinging my leg over Max. "You and Delta wore my ass out!"

"I think you wore me out," Max said as she kissed me softly. "I am going to take my shower," Max said as she eased out of bed.

I threw on one of Max's shirts and some panties before walking to the kitchen for some water. I could hear the shower running in the bathroom and Max singing. Colby was sitting on the couch when I walked through the living room.

"Sorry, Colby! I didn't think anyone was here," I said as I covered my panties by pulling the shirt down.

"Girl! What y'all do don't make any difference to me!" He snapped his fingers. "Happy Birthday!" At least earlier it sounded like it was a happy birthday." Colby grinned.

"Oh my God, Colby! Were we that loud?" I said as a blush came across my face.

Colby just grinned. "Just a little loud."

"Geesh, sorry, Colby."

"Girl, the way it sounded, there is nothing to be ashamed of. But who is Delta?"

"Um, Delta? I am not sure…. I don't know what you are talking about. Max is showering right now. Does she always sing in the shower?"

"Is Max singing?" Colby asked.

"Yes," I answered.

That was the first time she had sung since the breakdown. Colby clapped his hands together. "That is a good sign, Sadie, a really good sign."

I smile then scooted back to the bedroom. It was almost 6:00 when we both appeared in the living room. Colby closed his magazine back up. Shook his head and said, "Lesbians!"

"You are going to be late to your own dinner," Colby said as he threw his keys to Max. "You drive my SUV. I plan on getting lit tonight."

Max threw the keys back to Colby. "We will take my car. Sadie and I might leave early. Tori can bring your lit ass back home."

Everyone was at Larry's place by the time Max and I arrived. Tori was eating breadsticks, and Lacey was on the phone talking about a real estate deal. Zena was not there. We walked over joining the other two at the table. Lacey finally got off the phone after Tori elbowed her. Larry came over to talk to the group. He wished me a happy birthday before he took the group's order of two pizzas and wings with a pitcher of beer.

A 4x4 truck sat in the corner of the parking lot. The man inside grasped at the steering wheel as he watched Sadie through the window. The more she laughed, the tighter his grip got on the steering wheel. Blood was seeping through the white bandages.

The next stop was MadJax for some dancing. We all piled into the cars and headed out of Larry's parking lot. This was my first time at this location. I was excited to see where Colby worked. I looked at the huge neon sign as we entered the parking lot. "Wow! Looks like Las Vegas." Max came around helping me out of the car. Max grabbed my wrist smiling as she pulled me toward the entrance. The music was loud, and the dance floor was full already. A table opened, and Tori grabbed it quickly for the five of us. Colby bought a pitcher of beer for everyone. A slow dance came on, and Max stood up holding her hand out.

"Let's dance!" Max said to me. I placed my wrist in Max's hand, and she guided me to the dance floor. I wrapped my arms around Max's neck pressing my body against Max. We swayed back and forth slowly, unaware of anyone else on the floor, getting lost in kisses for moments at a time.

"You have changed my world, Max!" I whispered in Max's ear.

Max pulled me closer in the embrace. "I can say the same!"

I nibbled at Max's ear. "This has been such a great night. Everyone was so great, but all I can think about was your mouth on me, Max. Take me to Lover's Peak."

Max slipped her hands down to my ass. Max moaned in my ear. "Let's go!"

Max and I approached the table where Tori and Colby were guzzling down glasses of beer playing some game. Lacey looked bored as she was the designated driver.

"Thanks for the dinner guys but we are out of here," Max said.

"You just got here!" Colby chimed in.

"I know but let me see my choices…. Ummm…stay here with you drunks or have great sex with the sexy birthday lady!" Max smiled as I lightly punched Max in the arm.

"Thanks for everything guys," I said as Max started to pull me away.

Max pulled up to the wooden fence placing the car in park. The sky was clear, and stars could be seen from millions of miles away. Max and I climbed in the backseat. I laid down, and Max laid on top of me. Max was nibbling on my neck, and her hand slipped under my shirt cupping my breast. The nipples were hard as a rock and wanting to bust out of the bra. Max was already moaning as I let her hands move all over my body.

"I want you so bad!" Max moaned out.

Suddenly, the car jumped forward jolting us. The second hit came tossing Max onto the floorboard. Max scrambled back up. "What the fuck?" Max yelled out as the third hit came. The car jerked hard tossing us against the back of the front seats. Bright lights came beaming through the back window blinding us. As the truck backed up, I got the first glance of the hell that was in front of us.

"NO!" I screamed.

"Get out of the car, Mercedes!" The scream came from the truck driver over the revving engine.

"Stop it!" I screamed back. "Please!"

"Who the hell is that?" Max asked, but when she saw the fear in my eyes, she knew the answer. "Is it him? Sadie, damn it! Is it him?"

Mercedes! YOU HAVE THREE SECONDS TO GET OUT! He was screaming as loud as he could. "GET OUT BITCH! 3, 2, 1!"

Max looked over, "Who is Mercedes?" she said before the impact happened.

The truck slammed into the back of the car pushed it into a wooden fence. Cracks started to appear in the wood before the sound of it breaking could be heard in the car.

"Max!" I mouthed as the car tilted over the ledge.

"Hold on, Sadie!" Max yelled.

The car teetered for a moment before the front end finally dipped downward. The truck did one final push, and the rear of the car went over disappearing into the dark below. The man got out of the truck. Walking over to the edge, he looked down into complete darkness while he kicked the broken fence. He turned and slowly walking away. The truck turned around peeling out down the dirt road leaving a dust trail.

21

"I am not running because of you. I am running because of me…"
—Sadie

"Get up! Get up!" Zena screamed as she busted in Tori and Lacey's bedroom door. Tori sat straight up in bed followed by Lacey who almost fell out of bed from the loud screaming.

"What the fuck are you doing, Zena? How the hell do you have a key to our house?" Tori said as she covered Lacey's naked body with the blanket.

"Get the fuck up. Max has been in an accident." Zena was in a panic.

"What?" Lacey said as she reached over grabbing her shirt off the floor.

"Her car drove off Lover's Peak about two hours ago." Zena threw Tori's pants at her.

"How do you know that?" Tori said as she sat on the edge of the bed fumbling with the pants.

"Just hurry," Zena screamed.

"How in the fuck do you know that, Zena?" Tori was starting to panic.

"A state trooper called my phone. I guess they got my number from Max's phone. All I know was they were headed to the hospital with her and Sadie. We need to get there." Zena was pacing back and forth.

"I am drunk, so you or Lacey will have to drive," Tori said.

"I can't reach Colby. He is not home, and he is not answering his phone," Zena said as she started to cry.

"Let's go. We can try to reach him on the way to the hospital," Lacey said as she grabbed her car keys.

❧

I could hear the sirens and see the red flashing lights in the window of the ambulance. The lady paramedic was trying to ask me questions. I was trying to look around the paramedic to see Max, who was on the stretcher across from me. The other paramedic was working on Max trying to stop the bleeding. Blood was dripping down on the floor of the ambulance.

"Max! ... Max! Please, Max!" I was yelling.

The two paramedics stepped to the side long enough for me to see Max. She was so white, so pale and unconscious.

"Max, open your eyes baby! Is she okay? Is she okay?' I yelled at the paramedic as I tried to get up, but straps were holding me down. I screamed as a sharp pain ran through my side.

"Ma'am, please calm down. You will hurt yourself even more. They are doing all they can for her." The paramedic placed her hand on my shoulder. "Let them help her!"

I laid back, a stream of tears running down my cheek. "What the hell have I done?"

"Look! There is the ambulance," Lacey said as she sped the car up to get behind the ambulance. The speedometer was reading 80 miles per hour. Zena was in the back seat talking to Colby, who finally answered his phone. They were about five miles from the hospital.

"Colby is getting a ride in. He also sounded drunk. Did you have a party tonight?" Zena asked.

"We went out for Sadie's birthday," Tori answered. Lacey slapped at Tori's leg. Zena sat quietly in the backseat looking out the window for the rest of the ride.

Everyone jumped out of the car and ran toward the emergency room bay entrance. The ambulance doors flew open, and they could see Sadie come out first. She was awake and looking around trying to see Max.

"Check on Max!" I yelled as I was rolled through.

Max came out next. Lacey placed her hands over her mouth as she saw the stretcher roll off. Tori was screaming Max's name, and Zena stood back in a daze. The stretcher was covered in blood. Max was lifeless. The paramedics were calling out Max's stats to the doctors and nurses who had rushed out.

"Appears to be multiple broken bones, BP eighty over fifty, loss of blood due to puncture wound near the kidney area…" The stretcher disappeared through the doors leaving the three of them standing in the doorway alone.

Colby busted through the waiting room doors where Tori, Lacey and Zena was waiting for close to thirty minutes with no word yet. "What happened?" Colby said.

"The car went over Lover's Peak. We don't know why. We haven't heard anything on Max and Sadie, but Max looked bad coming in," Lacey said placing her arm on Colby's shoulder. A tear rolled down Colby's cheek.

Another thirty minutes passed by before the nurse walked into the waiting room. "Two of you can go see Ms. Jones now."

"How is Maxine Shields doing?" Tori asked as she stood up.

"She is in surgery. The doctor will be able to tell you more about Ms. Shields."

"You can follow me to Ms. Jones." The nurse said as she walked out the door with Tori and Colby on her heels.

As the door shut, Lacey turned around and walked over to Zena. "Have you lost your mind? What were you thinking barging into our house like that?" Lacey asked firmly.

"I am sorry, Lace. I was so upset," Zena said through the tears.

"About Max? Really? You have been warned, Zena." Lacey said.

Zena lowered her head crying. Her eyes were swollen and red. "I am so messed up."

Lacey stepped closer and rubbed Zena's shoulder softly. "Z, I am sorry. Stop crying." Lacey stepped closer laying her lips softly on Zena's. Zena responded back letting her tongue slip softly into Lacey's mouth. Lacey pulled away slowly. "Tori can't find out about us Z, at least not now. Tell her I gave you a key to let yourself in one day and forgot to get it back, but only if she asks. I love you, Zena."

"Okay, Lacey. I am sorry. I love you too!"

"It will be fine, sweetie" she smiled at Zena then kissing her cheek softly. "A little more time is all I need."

Tori and Colby walked into my hospital room. They noticed my face was bruising already. My eyes were closed until I heard the door open.

"How is Max? I asked groggily.

"She is in surgery, baby girl!" How are you?" Colby asked.

"I have broken ribs and umm...some cuts and bruises. I need to see Max." I tried to get out of the bed. I screamed in pain as Colby helped me lay back down.

"You can't see her right now. Just relax, Sadie!" Colby started rubbing my head.

"What happened, Sadie?" Tori asked.

I started to cry. "I don't know. A car hit us, and we went over."

"You see the car?"

"No!"

Two hours went by before the doctor walked into my room. "Ms. Jones, your cousin is out of surgery. She is in critical but stable condition. Her leg is shattered in three places, and the puncture wound nicked her kidney. She lost a lot of blood, but with time, we expect her to recover."

I covered my face and broke down. Colby wrapped his arms around me crying along with me.

"Thank you, doctor. Can we see her?" Tori asked.

"Not yet. Maybe in about an hour. She is still in recovery. Ms. Jones, we want you to stay a couple of days for observation," the doctor said as he headed for the door.

"Okay, thanks again doctor!" Tori yelled out. Tori looked over at me. "Cousins? That was fast thinking, Sadie."

There was a knock on the door before it creaked open." Ms. Jones, we need to ask a few questions. We will have to ask your friends to leave unless you authorize them to stay," the police officer said as he walked in.

"They can stay!" I answered.

"I am going to tell Lacey and Zena the news on Max. They are waiting in the café" Tori said as she stood up.

I gave the police the same story I had told Tori and Colby. I had to say a vehicle hit us because there were witnesses. If it had not been for the tree that stopped Max's car from plunging down the cliff and the people who called for help, Max and I would have died. I could only hope Max would tell the same story. I was scared to say it was my husband. He could come back if he found out we were not dead. As soon as the police left, the nurse walked back in to give me a shot of morphine. Colby said goodbye as I dozed off from the meds.

I moaned in pain as I shifted in the hospital bed. The clock on the wall read 4:30 am. I forced myself up to the side of the bed. "Fuck!" I yelled out in pain. I hit the button to call the nurse.

"I want to go to Maxine Shields's room!" I ordered.

"Ms. Jones, do you think you are up for that?"

"Yes. Take me now please!" I barked back.

"Let me get a wheelchair," the nurse said.

I rolled into the ICU, and there was Max laying lifeless in the hospital bed. She was still and very pale. Her leg was up on wires with rods in traction going through it. Tori was sleeping in the corner chair, and Colby was lying on the couch sound asleep. I reached over touching Max's hand softly. "I am sorry, baby!" I whispered as I laid my head down on the bed. "I don't know how he found out. God baby! Please be okay!" I cried silently. I turned Max's hand over and opened her fingers up. I laid my wrist in Max's palm. "Baby, grab my wrist!" Max's fingers were limp. I stood up just long enough to whisper in Max's ear. "Baby, I want you to grab my wrist!" Max's fingers remained limp. I slumped back down and buried my face in the bed crying silently. Suddenly, I felt Max's finger come to life, Max slowly closed her fingers around my wrist.

"Hey!" Max barely whispered.

"Hey, you!" I whispered back.

"You okay?"

"I am now!" I said with tears running down my cheek. I stood up again kissing Max softly on the temple. "I can't let him hurt you again!" Max closed her eyes and fell back to sleep.

The sun was coming through the windows. Tori and Colby were awake and watching a game show on the television. Max opened her eyes and winced in pain for a few seconds. She was trying to focus her eyes on the light in the room.

"Hey, bud!" Tori said.

Colby leaned over and kissed Max's forehead. "You scared the hell out of us!"

Lacey and Zena were at the end of the bed. "Hey lady!" Lacey called out.

"I need some water!" Colby held the straw to Max's lips for her to take a sip. "Where is Sadie?"

"In her room. I will go get her, Max."

Colby walked into Sadie's room to find the room clean and empty. A nurse was coming out of the bathroom.

"Where is the woman that was in this room?" Colby asked.

"She checked out earlier. We tried to stop her, but she insisted. She could barely walk." The nurse answered.

"Earlier?" Colby questioned.

"Yes. Are you...?" The nurse pulled a letter from her pocket. "Are you Max?"

Colby looked at the letter addressed to Max. He hesitated before answering, "Oh yes, I am Max!"

"She left this for you," the nurse said as she handed the letter to Colby. "Oh, and this." The nurse handed Colby an hourglass.

Colby walked back into the room carrying the letter and the hourglass. Max looked over at Colby. "What is the matter, Colby? Where is Sadie?"

"Sadie has checked out but left this for you."

"Read it!" Max ordered as she held the hourglass turning it over watching the sand fall.

Colby cleared his voice before he opened the letter unfolding it slowly.

Dear Max,

What we had the past month, I never knew existed in this world. I have learned to love and to feel. It is amazing. I love you, Maxine. Please never forget that. I am not running because of you. I am running because of me. I need to fix my past before I can be yours one hundred percent. The thought of you or your friends getting hurt because of me is something I can't live with. I can't put you in danger again. We were lucky we were not killed. I am sorry, baby. I hope I can come back to you one day but till then open up to your friends. Let them in like you let me in. I love you, and so does your friends, Max.

All my love,
Sadie.

Max closed her eyes, and the tears rolled down her cheek. "Sadie!" she whispered as she broke down in heaves. "NO! NO!" Max was starting to rock the bed as she began to thrash.

Tori sat down at the top trying to brace her head. "Max, calm down!"

Colby sat beside her arms trying to hold them down. Lacey and Zena both laid their hands on Max's thrashing leg rubbing it gently. Max finally laid still as she broke down completely. Tori rubbed her head as Max buried her face.

"Sadie! No Sadie!" Max's cries filled the room.

"We are here, Max. We got you!" Tori said as she held Max tightly.

With the hourglass in Max's hand, the last grain of sand dropped to the bottom.

❧

The woman leaned on the counter at the bus station. Her head was drooping, and she was barely able to stand. The man behind the counter looked around scared waiting for her to say something. Finally, he spoke to break the silence,

"Ma'am, are you okay?"

"I need a ticket to Sea Grove, New York."

"Okay, round trip?" the young man asked.

"No, one way," the woman whispered with her head still drooping.

"Name on the ticket, ma'am?"

The woman just held her head down letting the counter hold her body up.

"I have to have a name for the ticket," the young man repeated.

Lifting her head, the hair falling away from her face, the whites of her eyes filled with blood, she stared into his eyes. She inhaled and her face twisting in pain, her swollen lips whispering three words.

"Mercedes… Mercedes Hart…."

END

CPSIA information can be obtained
at www.ICGtesting.com
Printed in the USA
FFOW04n1446210518
46706627-48852FF